BEST
FRIENDS
GETTING SORTED

Rosie Rushton lives in Northampton. She took up writing because it gave her a wonderful excuse not to do the dusting and because the word processor was the only thing in the house that didn't answer back. Her three daughters managed to attain adulthood despite having the most embarrassing mother in Northamptonshire. She is passionately interested in family and relationship issues.

In addition to writing teenage fiction and running workshops in schools around the country, Rosie writes a weekly column for her local paper, contributes to a variety of national and local radio stations and writes travel features for national magazines, a somewhat remarkable feat for one who gets lost in a multi-storey carpark. Her two greatest ambitions are to write children's drama for television and see her first adult novel published before she is too old to look good in the publicity photographs.

Other books by Rosie Rushton, published by Piccadilly Press:

Best Friends – Together

Poppy

Olivia

Sophie

Melissa

Just Don't Make a Scene, Mum!

I Think I'll Just Curl Up and Die

How Could You Do This to Me, Mum?

Where Do We Go From Here?

Speak for Yourself

Staying Cool, Surviving School

You're My Best Friend, I Hate You!

BEST

FRIENDS

GETTING SORTED

ROSIE RUSHTON

PICCADILLY PRESS • LONDON

For all the pupils of Whitley Bay High School
and Northampton Middle School, and for Anna, Lucinda,
Kirsty, Sam, the two Matthews, Andrew and Chris –
for being so inspiring!

Text copyright © Rosie Rushton, 1999
Cover photographs © Ute Klaphake, 1998

Printed and bound by WBC, Bridgend
for the publishers Piccadilly Press Ltd.,
5 Castle Road, London NW1 8PR

A catalogue record for this book is available
from the British Library

1 3 5 7 9 10 8 6 4 2

ISBNs: 1 85340 596 5 (trade paperback)
1 85340 502 7 (hardback)

Designed by Judith Robertson
Cover design by Mandy Sherliker

Chapter 1

DARK SECRETS

"IT'S USELESS! I can't do it!"

Chloë Sanderson ripped the page from her exercise book, scrunched it into a ball and flung it at the wastepaper basket. It missed and joined the other dozen attempts at 'King Lear – A Man More Sinned Against than Sinning?' on the pale blue carpet.

Terrific. Half of Sunday wasted and nothing to show for it. She could just imagine what Mrs Reilly would say on Monday morning if the requisite two sides of A4 were not lying on her desk. The new English teacher was hardly charm personified at the best of times; on Friday, when she had returned Chloë's essay, she had been even more sarcastic than usual.

"I was led to believe," she had declared, jutting out her bony little chin and wrinkling her nose as if just catching a whiff of rotting fish, "that you were one of the more able of Year Eleven students. On this showing, I have been misinformed. What has gone wrong?"

What has gone right? Chloë had wanted to shout. My

mother threw my father out and now she works like a maniac all week and falls apart all over the place every weekend; my dad keeps phoning and asking me if I miss him, and I say no, even though it's a lie, because it can't be right to miss someone who hits your mum every few months; and the guy I love to distraction hasn't replied to any of my letters or e-mails. Somehow your dumb essay doesn't seem important by comparison.

Of course, she hadn't said any of that. She could never say half the things that were rattling round in her head. It was OK for people like Nick Bowen; everyone felt sorry for him, what with his dad dying like that and leaving them with no money. If he had a bad day, or stormed off in a huff, people made allowances. No one would make allowances for her, simply because no one knew. She was used to keeping her mouth shut on the subject of her father's violence; used to pretending that life was hunky-dory. After all, she had been doing it since she was six years old. She hated him for the fact that she had to tell lies all the time, make out that he was away on a business trip when all the time he was living in a hotel because her mum couldn't take any more.

Not, of course, that he was always like that; most of the time he was really nice and loving and funny and . . .

"Stop it!" Chloë shouted out loud to the empty room, running her fingers distractedly through her crinkly auburn hair. If she wasn't careful, she would start thinking like Mum. That was why she still hadn't finished the essay that old Reilly had insisted on her rewriting; because she'd spent so much time trying to get her mother to see sense.

It had started on Friday when she got home from school

to find her mother standing in the sitting-room, arranging a huge vase of orchids.

"Darling!" Suzy had thrown open her arms to hug Chloë, and she noticed that her mother seemed brighter than she had been for days. "Good day at school?"

"No," Chloë had replied. "What's with the flowers? Another besotted fan, I suppose?"

As Pennine TV's highest profile presenter, her mother was constantly receiving cards and gifts from viewers whose lives were so sad that they didn't have anything better to spend their money on.

"No," Suzy had said, shaking her head. "Actually, they're from Dad. Look!"

She had thrust a card into Chloë's hand.

My dearest darling Suzy,
Believe me when I say I love you totally. I am so, so sorry for everything. Please forgive me, sweetheart. I miss you so.
Your own Teddy Bear.

Chloë had felt her chest tighten.

"Yuck!" She had thrown the card on to the sofa. "You're not really going to be taken in by all that sentimental drivel, are you? He always says he's sorry after the event."

Her mum had turned away and begun fiddling with a leaf. "I know, I know, but maybe this time . . ."

"Mum!" Chloë had struggled to keep her temper. "You said that last time, and the time before. And what happened? You ended up covered in bruises and . . ."

"But I've never thrown him out before," interrupted her mother. "When we spoke on the phone yesterday, he said it had really brought him to his senses, made him realise what he stood to lose. He begged me to have him back."

Chloë's hazel eyes widened and her mouth dropped open.

"No!" The word was out before she could stop it. "Can't you see? Don't you have any sense? He'll come back, and it will all be fine for a bit, and then he'll start getting moody, and we'll get the long silences and then one day, you'll say one word out of place and he'll thump you!"

She choked on the words. Just remembering how it had been always made her feel sick.

"Are you blind, Mum? Can't you see that?"

"Yes, yes, yes!" Her mother had wheeled round, her eyes full of tears. "I can see the sense, I can see the logic, I know what I *ought* to do – but I miss him, for God's sake! I really, really miss him!"

And with that she had rushed out of the room and up the spiral staircase, slamming her bedroom door behind her. Chloë had started to run up after her, but stopped halfway. What was there to say? It had all been said a hundred times before.

Of course, her mum had come down later and said Chloë was quite right and she had to be strong and see things for what they really were; and Chloë had hugged her and said she wouldn't go out with her mates that evening, so they could have a cosy evening in; to which her mum had replied that of course she must go and she was planning on an early night anyway.

"I think it's great that you've got this new bunch of

friends, darling," Suzy had said with a wan smile as she rubbed her swollen eyes. "At least you're not pining away for that Jack Kempton any more."

Which just showed how little she knew, Chloë thought now, flicking her hair out of her face and writing the essay title at the top of yet another clean page. Not a day went by without her thinking about Jack, about the way he had held her, told her how much he loved her and promised to write every week. When the letters never came, her mum had said that all holiday romances bit the dust sooner or later and that things said in the moonlight on a Greek beach weren't to be taken seriously – but Chloë just knew there had to be a reason for Jack's silence. Her friend Jasmin agreed; when he failed to reply to the e-mail they sent from the new computer at Mr Johnson's café, Jasmin said Jack had probably been transferred to another holiday centre, what with him being such a mega good sailing instructor; when he forgot to send Chloë a birthday card, Jasmin explained that the Greek postal service was known for its unreliability. Chloë had a sneaking feeling that Jasmin was simply trying to make her feel better, but it was more comfortable to believe her than to think about the alternative.

The shrilling of the telephone interrupted her thoughts. Jack! It could be Jack! She had read about things like that; you think really deeply about someone close to you and they pick up the vibes and phone you. People wrote books about it and she had been trying it for weeks, willing him to phone. Maybe this was it; maybe it had finally worked.

She jumped up from her desk, knocking her pencil-case

on to the floor, and dashed out of the bedroom and down the stairs. She was halfway down when she heard her mother's voice, talking on the kitchen extension.

"Two-four-five, seven-one-seven-one, Suzy Sanderson. I'm sorry, I can't hear you. It seems to be a bad line."

A bad line! Greece! It was Jack!

"Oh. You want to speak to Chloë? Well, look, I'm not sure that's a good idea right now . . ."

Chloë crashed into the kitchen. "Mum!"

Her mother held up a hand and mouthed something incomprehensible.

"Well, actually, we're about to eat lunch and . . ."

What was she on? How dare she block her calls!

"Mum! I'm here! Give me the phone!"

Suzy clamped her hand over the mouthpiece. "Chloë, wait . . ."

"Give me the phone!" Chloë snatched the receiver from her mother's hand.

Her mother sighed and began hovering anxiously at her side. Chloë waved a hand and gestured her to go away.

"Hi!" she breathed as huskily as she could down the phone. "It's Chloë here."

She closed her eyes and imagined Jack, bronzed and muscular, standing in the lobby at the Skiathos Sailing Club, waited for his deep, gravelly voice to send those little shivers of delight down her spine.

"Oh Chloë, Chloë! Darling, I've missed you so much!"

The words were right but the voice was wrong.

Chloë felt sick with a mixture of disappointment and anger and a longing for the way things might have been.

"Dad." Her voice was flat.

"Oh Chloë . . ." Her father's voice cracked with emotion. Chloë's heart lurched; he sounded dreadful.

"What?" He was obviously calling from his mobile phone and she strained to catch what he was saying. "Supper? Tonight?"

Out of the corner of her eye, Chloë could see her mum gesturing frantically in her direction. For just a moment, she hesitated.

It would be nice to see him, just to make sure he was OK. It had been four weeks now, and after all, he was her dad and she did love him, despite everything. And maybe Mum was right, maybe this time things would be different.

"Well, I . . ."

As she glanced at her mother for approval, Suzy turned and Chloë saw the yellow, fading bruise on the side of her mum's neck.

She gripped the receiver more tightly.

"No, Dad. I don't want to see you."

She took a deep breath and willed herself not to cry.

"Not tonight. Not tomorrow. I don't want to see you ever again."

Chapter 2

SO MUCH FOR MAKING PLANS . . .

She wasn't going to come.

She didn't want to see him.

Sanjay Fraser glanced at his watch for the tenth time in two minutes and hunched his shoulders against the cold November wind. He wasn't surprised; after all it had been a dumb idea in the first place. And yet, when he'd suggested it on Friday Jasmin had seemed really keen. But then again, she probably only said yes to get him off her back.

Sanjay kicked a stray Coke can into the gutter and leaned against the wall of the City Museum, idly watching a couple of guys stringing Christmas lights over the lampposts. Now that he was here he felt a complete jerk. What had he been thinking of? Cool guys didn't invite girls to exhibitions; they took them to discos or movies, they bought them popcorn and held their hands in the back row. Sanjay had never held a girl's hand before he met Jasmin, and he had been rather looking forward to the opportunity of doing it again.

He should have guessed that she had no intention of coming by the way she had reacted when he suggested picking her up from home.

"No!" she had exclaimed. "No, honestly, don't do that. I'll meet you in town."

"It's no trouble," he had urged her. "It will mean I can spend longer with you."

He had thought that, for him, that was a pretty cool remark. Jasmin obviously hadn't thought so.

"I said no, OK!"

He had been pretty gobsmacked – Jasmin wasn't the moody type, that was one of the things he liked about her. Of course, now it was all perfectly clear. She had never had any intention of coming in the first place, which was why she hadn't wanted him to turn up at the café.

And to think that he had imagined that finally his luck was changing. He had never been very good with people but Jasmin was different. At Chloë's party, she had been so easy to talk to and hadn't seemed to mind that he was the smallest guy in the year and hopeless at small talk. They had gone out in a gang lots of times since, but it had taken him until now to pluck up the courage to ask her out on her own and now he wished he hadn't. At least before he could pretend that one day they would be an item; now he was almost certain they wouldn't.

He'd give her five more minutes and then he would go in. It wouldn't be the same without her, but it was too good an opportunity to pass up, Jasmin or no Jasmin – an entire exhibition devoted to animation and cartoons. The newspaper had said that there would even be experts on hand from some of the best studios; if he could just get to talk to one of them, find out the best way to get on one of the animation degree courses, that would be so cool.

Who was he kidding? His parents would go ballistic if he told them what he really wanted to do with his life. It had been bad enough today, what with his dad going on and on about the fact that his grades in Maths were dropping, and demanding to know why he needed to go out again when he had been bowling on Friday. As if fun had to be rationed – not that his father would recognise fun if it leaped up and hit him in the face.

He couldn't win; his mother, despite having lived in England for twenty years, still thought like a traditional Hindu, and believed she had the right to vet all his friends for him, and all his father wanted was for Sanjay to make it to Cambridge and Harvard and become a high-flying lawyer or some stuffy academic like himself. What Sanjay wanted didn't seem to matter much to either of them.

He took one last, long look up and down The Headrow. There was no sign of Jasmin. Perhaps he should phone her, in case she really had just forgotten. But if she had, it meant that it wasn't important to her, and right now he didn't want to know that.

"Sanjay Fraser!" A hearty thump on his shoulder blades nearly knocked Sanjay off his feet. "Here for the exhibition, are you? Splendid, splendid – just the ticket!"

Sanjay turned to find himself staring into the somewhat spotty but frightfully enthusiastic face of Mr Buckley, his IT teacher from Lockbridge High.

"Oh – er, hello, sir," he stuttered, casting one more furtive glance down the street. "No – well, yes, but . . ."

"Me too," enthused Mr Buckley. "Just up your street, isn't it, all this 3-D animation stuff? Thought I ought to come along – got to keep pace with my star pupil, eh?"

He roared with laughter and Sanjay gave a wan smile.

"Well, well," cried Mr Buckley, "let's go in, shall we? No point hanging about here in the cold."

Sanjay's heart sank. Mr Buckley was a pretty OK sort as teachers went, but spending an afternoon in his company was not at all what he had had in mind.

"Well, actually, I – that is . . ." Sanjay began. And stopped. What was the point? Jasmin wasn't going to turn up. She had probably forgotten he existed.

And at least Mr Buckley wouldn't think he was weird for wanting to spend Sunday at an exhibition.

He turned, threw one last, lingering glance down the street and followed Mr Buckley into the museum.

———

"You can't do this to me, Mum! It's just not fair!"

Jasmin Johnson stood in the doorway of the kitchen, her dark eyes flashing with anger as she glared at her mother.

"Believe me, love, life is rarely fair," sighed her mum, handing her a pile of menus. "And will you please keep your voice down? The whole café can hear you."

"That's only because the place is half empty," retorted Jasmin, banging the menus down on the counter top. "You don't need me any longer; you're only finding jobs for me to do because you can't bear to see me going out and having a good time!"

"Oh, Jasmin, grow up!" Her mother sighed with exasperation and ran her fingers through her jet-black, braided hair. "You were out on Friday night, you went shopping all afternoon yesterday . . ."

"Oh sorry! I didn't realise you were keeping a time sheet!"

"And now just when I ask you to spare me a couple of hours of your time you announce that you're swanning off again. And you have the nerve to tell me I'm the unfair one!"

"But, Mum, I promised San . . . My mates!" Jasmin corrected herself just in time. Her mother, as well as being a complete slave driver, had very outmoded views on dating.

"Well, you will just have to un-promise them, won't you?" retorted her mother, whose use of the English language was colourful in the extreme. "It's Jenny Bowen's day off, Delia's phoned in sick and that Melanie is as good as useless. I need you here."

"Oh, Josie, let the child go!" Jasmin's father looked up from the cooker, where he was doing something exotic with tiger prawns and root ginger. "We'll manage."

"You mean, *I'll* manage!" her mother retorted, wheeling round to face him and almost knocking a plate of couscous on to the floor. "It's all very well for you – I don't see you rushing out front to serve the customers and clear tables and tot up the bills and . . ."

"You know I can't face that sort of thing these days," her father began, shaking spices into the saucepan.

"Can't? Or won't?" her mother demanded, the gold bangles on her wrist jangling as she gestured furiously. "The accident was nearly two years ago, Harry; you can't hide away for ever, you know. This whole thing was your idea; I said it was crazy . . ."

"Josie, don't start. Please." Harry sounded weary.

His wife ignored him. "Anyway, why shouldn't Jasmin

pull her weight? She'll only be mooching about town wasting time."

"I won't!" Jasmin scowled at her mother. "We're going to a museum, actually."

Her mum's eyes widened in astonishment. "A museum? You?" She appeared as surprised as if Jasmin had announced that she was intending to spend the afternoon abseiling down a cliff-face with the Royal Marines. "I thought you hated that sort of thing."

Jasmin shrugged. "It's for a school project," she lied. "But it doesn't matter; I'll just tell Mrs Braithwaite I had to work all day for my parents."

"You will do no such thing!" her father expostulated, dropping his wooden spoon in horror.

"Don't you dare!" cried her mother at the same moment.

Bull's-eye! thought Jasmin.

Her father wiped his hands on a tea towel and turned to face her. "You go, love – I guess I can do a short stint on the cash desk."

He moved reluctantly towards the door, his hand going instinctively to his face to cover the long, silvery scar that snaked its way from his left eye to the corner of his mouth. Jasmin felt a pang of sympathy for him.

"Are you sure, Dad?"

"Of course I'm sure!" he affirmed with a lopsided smile. "We're just glad that you are taking your schoolwork so seriously – aren't we, Josephine?"

"I guess," sighed her mother, eyeing Jasmin just a little suspiciously.

"Thanks, Mum! Thanks, Dad!"

Jasmin's guilt was swiftly swallowed up in a great wave of relief. She sped upstairs to the flat, grabbed her jacket and ran through the café, glancing up at the clock as she went. Two-fifteen. She was late already.

Sanjay would think she had forgotten.

As if, she thought, running along Millers Lane. When someone asks you out on a date for the first time in your entire life, you tend not to forget. She had been really excited when he'd asked her; even though Chloë had thought the whole thing hysterical.

"He's asked you to a museum?" she had gasped, bursting out laughing. "But that's so boring!"

"No it's not!" Jasmin had said defensively. "It'll be interesting. I want to find out more about all this computer stuff he does."

She hadn't added that she would be happy to spend the whole afternoon watching paint dry if it meant being near Sanjay.

And she hadn't said a word about it to anyone else. She didn't want people to think there was anything in it, just in case he never asked her anywhere else again.

And she certainly didn't want her parents to get wind of who she was spending her time with. They would be sure to flip.

And it wouldn't just be because Sanjay was a boy.

Chapter 3

POST MORTEM
ON A MESS-UP

SUNDAYS, thought Nick Bowen, idly zapping through the TV channels, were the absolute pits. There was nothing to do, nowhere to go – just the four walls of his gran's poky little house closing in on him. He hated it so much; hated the cramped rooms overstuffed with dark mahogany furniture, the dreary little back garden with its naff garden gnome and shell-shaped birdbath. All his life he had been used to space and light and here he felt as if he were slowly suffocating.

His mum had said that living with his grandmother was just temporary, somewhere to stay until they got their lives sorted; but it had been nearly four months now, and if they didn't move out soon, he thought he would go mad. Madder than I am already, that is, he thought, punching the volume button angrily. 'The Flintstones' theme tune blared into the tiny sitting-room. It was a stupid programme but it was something to watch – and it helped to blot out the miserable thoughts that kept chasing one another round and round inside his head.

For just a while, a few weeks back, he had actually dared to believe that he was getting over it all. Not forgetting, of course – he knew he would never forget. But after Chloë Sanderson's party, when he had plucked up the courage to ask her out to the cinema and she had actually said yes, it felt as if something good was going to happen after the months of misery. Of course, he hadn't planned for Jasmin and Sinead and Sanjay to string along too, but even so, it had been a laugh, and Nick had begun to feel he belonged. Now, after what had happened on Friday, he wondered if he ever would again.

He hurled the remote control on to the floor and thumped his fist into one of the tapestry cushions on the sagging sofa. What the hell was wrong with him? Guys of sixteen didn't go round blubbing their eyes out, just because they'd seen some dumb poster in a restaurant window. It wouldn't have mattered so much if he had been on his own, but for once it had looked as if he might get Chloë to himself for a bit. And like a jerk, he'd blown it.

They had all been bowling and everything had gone really well. He had played on top form, had a real laugh and even come out with some witty one-liners that had the others in hysterics, probably because they had never seen him so laid back. And then someone – Sinead, he thought it was – had suggested they all pooled their cash and went for a pizza. At the time, it had seemed like a great idea.

Tuscany – The Place Where Dreams Come True, that's what the poster in the window of Pizza Palace had said. Just thinking about those words had made him clench his fist and bang it into his thigh.

"Nick?" Chloë had looked at him with concern. "Are you OK?"

"Fine," he had said, biting his lip. "Just cold."

Only it was a lie. He hadn't been cold and he hadn't been fine. He had a lump in his throat and a tight band across his chest; his legs had felt as if they were turning to jelly. As the others started checking their purses and working out whether they could afford to share a Giant Geronimo Deep Dish Supreme, he found himself unable to tear his eyes away from the picture of Tuscan hills and olive groves and that little whitewashed farmhouse that reminded him so heart-wrenchingly of his old home.

And as Chloë grabbed his arm and dragged him towards the door, his heart had begun racing and all he could hear in his head were his dad's words.

"I love this place, Nick," he had said. "I don't ever want to go back to England. I want to stay here for ever."

Well, you managed it, didn't you? he had thought angrily, shaking himself free of Chloë's grip. It's all right for you; you'll be over there for ever and Mum and me will be left to cope with this awful mess on our own.

"I'm going to make a fortune, son, renovating these old farmhouses." That's what his dad had said, over and over again. "You'll see – we've got a great future ahead of us here."

What fortune? What future? Nick had almost said the words out loud. And that was when it had happened. To his horror, his eyes had filled with tears and a strangled sob caught in his throat.

"You go in with the others, I'll catch you in a minute." He had practically shoved Chloë through the door, desperate to get away before the tears spilled over.

"Nick, where are you going? What's . . . ?"

He had left her staring after him as he had run, head down, along the street and round the first corner. He had kept running until his breath was coming in short, sharp gasps and then he had flopped down on a bench and buried his head in his hands.

"Dad! Oh Dad!"

He hadn't realised that he had said the words out loud until an elderly lady in a green plastic rain hat had tapped his arm and asked him if he needed help.

Of course, he'd got up then, stuffed his hands in his pockets and started walking back to the pizzeria. But in the end he simply couldn't face it; couldn't bring himself to answer all their questions, explain that seeing that poster made him think yet again of his dad's grave, stark and white and new in the tiny churchyard in a remote Italian village. So he had simply kept on walking until he got home. And, he was quite sure, blown it big-time with Chloë.

"Right, that's the washing-up done!" His thoughts were interrupted by his grandmother bustling into the room.

"Mum's just making the coffee and . . ." She stopped dead at the sight of the flickering television screen. "Goodness me, you don't want to be slumped here in front of all this rubbish!"

She leaned forward and switched it off with an exasperated sigh. "Haven't you got anything better to do with your afternoon?"

"Like what?" Nick grunted, deliberately switching it back on again, even louder than before.

"Well, there must be heaps of things," replied his gran briskly, her forehead creasing in a frown as she tried desperately to think of something. "Model making, you used to like that."

"Gran, that was when I was ten years old," muttered Nick.

"Well, why not kick a ball about in the fresh air, then? It'll do you good – you're looking very peaky these days."

She laid a hand anxiously on his forehead. Nick jerked his head away in irritation. "Don't fuss, Gran. I'm fine."

Why couldn't she stop treating him like a kid and just leave him alone?

"Well, you don't look fine to me and I do think . . . oh, there you are, Jenny dear!" She broke off as Nick's mum appeared in the doorway, balancing a tray of coffee cups.

"Nick!" She dumped the tray on the occasional table. "You're not gawping at that television again, are you?"

Jenny slumped down in the armchair opposite him. "Can't you find something better to do?"

"Don't you start!" Nick snapped.

His mum took a deep breath, bit her lip and forced a smile. "I thought you said you were going out with your mates today?"

"Yes, well I changed my mind, didn't I?" Nick jumped to his feet. "I didn't realise I had to file a report on my every movement."

He knew he was being off with her, but right now he didn't need to be reminded of his original plans. He had intended to ask Chloë to go ice-skating – he had had rather enjoyable fantasies about holding her hand and wrapping his arm round her waist – but after the way he had behaved on Friday, he knew it would be pointless. She would just laugh in his face.

"I didn't mean that, I just thought . . ." began his mother.

23

"Well, don't, OK?"

"Nick!"

"Sorry." He hated himself for being so moody. It wasn't like him – he had never been like that before. He touched her arm. "Sorry, Mum, all right?"

"All right."

His mum ruffled his hair and although every nerve in his body was jangling, he made himself stand still and smile back. It wasn't her fault that she had the biggest dweeb in town for a son.

"I've got it!" exclaimed his gran, cutting in on his thoughts and clapping her hands as enthusiastically as if she had just discovered a way of mending the hole in the ozone layer. "You could make a start on decorating your room. I've got scrapers and paint stripper somewhere and . . ."

"No!" The moment he had snapped back and seen his grandmother's face cloud with disappointment, Nick regretted it. His gran meant well; he had complained often enough about the grotty floral wallpaper and brown skirting-boards in the cramped little bedroom. But to start redecorating would be like admitting that he was here to stay. And he couldn't bear that.

"I mean, it's not worth it, Gran," he said, using all his energy to muster up another smile. "Mum and I will be getting our own place soon, after all."

"It's going to be some time before we can do that, I'm afraid," sighed his mum, taking a sip of coffee. "I never realised how expensive property is around here."

"But, Mum, you promised!" he cried. "You said by Christmas . . ."

"It's not Mum's fault, love," interjected his gran. "She's doing her best, working all hours at the café, but these things take time. Of course, if your father hadn't left her with all those debts . . ."

That did it.

"That's right, lay into Dad again!" Nick grabbed his grey fleece from the back of the chair and pulled it over his head. "He did his best, you know – it's not his fault he died before the money started coming in. Whatever you may think," he added.

He could feel the anger rising up inside him, felt his fingernails digging into the palms of his hands. He pushed past them into the narrow hallway. His mum followed on his heels.

"Nick? Gran didn't mean it like that, love."

Nick said nothing but yanked open the front door. He knew quite well what his grandmother meant.

"Where are you going?"

His mum's face creased with concern and Nick noticed how weary and drawn she looked. It was true; she was working too hard.

He took a deep breath and gave her a quick hug.

"I guess I'll go for a run," he said. "Get some of that fresh air you're both so keen on!"

He was rewarded with a broad grin from his mother.

"You could run to the DIY store," called his gran. "Pick up some paint and . . ."

"OK, Gran," he replied placatingly. "Perhaps I will."

Just leave me alone, he thought, slamming the door and breaking into a fast run along Talbot Street. When he'd been captain of cross-country at his old school, Benham Grange, running had always been his way of getting rid of a bad mood – not that pounding along these damp pavements overshadowed by grimy buildings could compare with the rolling Sussex downland dotted with sheep and blazing gorse bushes.

But it was better than sitting in the house thinking. Anything was better than that.

He wheeled round the corner and headed for the canal, picking up speed as the road sloped down towards the waterfront.

He felt so angry; not just about the way his life had been turned upside-down or having to listen to Gran criticising everything his father had done, but with his dad for dying like that, abandoning him when he needed him most. People had assured him that the grief would pass with time, but no one had mentioned this all-consuming rage that made him act like a total dork.

As he reached the waterfront, he slowed to a halt and sank down on one of the benches overlooking the busy canal. It wasn't that he was exhausted; he was used to running twelve kilometres every Saturday afternoon.

It was simply that he couldn't see where he was going through the blur of tears.

Chapter 4

THE THINGS WE DO FOR LOVE

ANSWER IT. Please, please answer it.

Engaged.

Sinead Flaherty hurled the portable phone on to her bed and glanced at her watch. Seventeen hours and thirty-five minutes to go. Seventeen hours and thirty-five minutes until she saw him again. It seemed like for ever.

She fancied him something chronic. Not that it got her anywhere; everyone could see that Nick Bowen only had eyes for Chloë. Which wasn't surprising, since Chloë was slim and willowy and pretty and totally together; everything, in fact, that Sinead knew she would never be.

She redialled the number but it was still engaged. He was probably chatting to Chloë right now, laughing and giggling, inviting her out, even. Maybe they were out already, checking out the stalls at Granary Wharf, sipping coffee, holding hands.

They'd better not be holding hands.

She looked at her watch again. Seventeen and a half hours exactly. Not that Nick was the only reason she wanted the week to start; even five days of hard slog at Lockbridge High was preferable to being at home right now.

When her mum had come into all that money and they had moved from what the newspapers called "the infamous Burnthedge estate" to this posh waterfront apartment in the same block as Chloë, she had thought that life would be a blast; but what with a mother who divided her time between mooning around saying she was homesick and dashing about wielding dusters and polishing everything in sight, a father who was more keen on painting flowers on tables and giraffes on bookcases than sorting his wife out, and a holier-than-thou kid sister who made the Pope look like a tearaway, getting through the weekend in one piece was like negotiating a minefield while wearing a blindfold.

That's why she had been so keen to make Friday evening last as long as possible; why she had suggested going for a pizza once the bowling was finished. Not that she would have bothered at all had she known that Nick was going to bunk off like that – it had cost her three pounds fifty, and all for nothing. To be fair, Chloë did keep telling her that she wasn't interested in Nick, that she was in love with this Jack guy, but Sinead wasn't stupid. Jack never materialised and Nick was on the spot, hanging on Chloë's every word. It would only be a matter of time before Chloë realised that a boy in the hand was worth two on a Greek island and then she would flutter those obscenely long eyelashes at Nick and any remote chance Sinead had would bite the dust.

But then again, she thought, picking up the phone and punching in Nick's number, if he had been that keen on Chloë, he wouldn't have dashed off without a word. Would he? At first they had thought he must have left something behind at the Superbowl, but then Sanjay said he thought it was because of them going to an Italian restaurant. She didn't believe that. After all, his dad had been dead for months now, and besides, Nick ate pizza for school lunch as if it was going out of fashion.

Perhaps Nick was in some kind of trouble. Perhaps he needed a shoulder to cry on. She conjured up a vision of herself sitting close to his side, holding his hand while he confided his deepest secrets. She had just got to the bit where he touched her cheek and told her that she was the most understanding person he had ever known when she realised that his number was actually ringing.

She slammed it down in alarm. What could she say? "Hi, Nick, I was just wondering if you got back OK on Friday"? Get real – it hardly showed her compassionate nature, since it was already Sunday afternoon.

"Sinead! Have you got the phone?"

Her mother flung open her bedroom door. "How many times have I told you to leave the phone in the sitting-room where it belongs?"

She snatched it out of Sinead's hand and began rubbing at it frantically with a duster from her apron pocket.

"Mum! For heaven's sake . . ."

"Look, you've made it all sticky – and besides, you should be doing your homework, not wasting time . . ."

Homework! That was it!

Sinead fixed a penitent yet conscientious expression on her face. "Sorry, Mum," she said meekly, "but I was phoning one of my friends about our French homework.

I'm trying so hard to get a better grade this term and there's one bit that I just can't do."

She paused, aware of how crucial it was to get the timing just right. And then she sighed. "But I guess," she said with a weak smile, "I'll just have to settle for a B instead of an A."

Her mother frowned and then handed the phone back to her. "OK," she said, "but be quick about it. I need to call your father and remind him that we're eating at six. Always assuming," she added, "that he remembers he has a home and a family."

Don't let's start that again, thought Sinead, grabbing the phone and punching in Nick's number yet again. Ever since her dad had chucked in his job at the factory and set up his furniture workshop, her mum had been edgy about his every move. And ever since her mother had become fanatical about keeping the house clean, Sinead had noticed, her dad spent more and more time away from it.

Answer. Please answer.

Oh my God, they're answering.

"Hello?" It was a woman's voice.

"May I speak to Nick, please?"

Her heart pounded in anticipation as the woman at the other end gabbled on. Apparently it was his gran, and she was ever so sorry but Nick, bless him, wasn't there.

"He's out?"

Her heart sank. She had been right; he'd taken Chloë out.

"He's what? Gone for a run?"

Perhaps he wasn't with Chloë. She didn't seem the running sort.

"He's gone *where*?"

She rammed a finger into her left ear to blot out the sounds of her mother's frantic vacuuming.

"The *DIY store*?"

He was most definitely not with Chloë.

"Oh, a message. Yes, could you tell him that . . . no. No, it's OK, thanks. I'll leave it."

She banged the phone down and yanked open her wardrobe. Scrabbling among the heap of shoes on the bottom shelf, she pulled out her trainers and stuffed her feet into them.

She grabbed a sweatshirt from her chest of drawers and picked up her French book.

"Mum!" she called, squirting herself with a generous amount of Anais Anais. "The phone's all yours – I'm just going over to . . ."

She paused. "To Jasmin's. To work on this French. OK?"

Her mother, looking flushed and dishevelled, stuck her head round the dining-room door.

"It's freezing out there," she said. "Why not pop up to the Sandersons' flat and ask Chloë instead?"

Sinead thought fast. "She's useless at French," she lied. "And besides, the fresh air will do me good."

As a parting shot, it was a winner. Her mother was too stunned to move a muscle, let alone speak.

"See you!"

Sinead slammed the door and sped down the stairs. For the first time in her life, a trip to Mega DIY seemed the coolest way to spend a Sunday afternoon.

It was amazing what you would do for love.

In the flat above, Chloë was biting her fingernails and trying very hard not to cry with frustration.

It was no good – she couldn't write a single word. Her brain felt like cotton wool and all she could think about was how her dad had sounded on the phone, how he was now probably sitting in his hotel room feeling lonely and unloved.

Stop it. He deserves it.

But then again, he didn't have anyone else – just her and Mum.

And work had been going badly for him.

And Christmas was only six weeks away.

Families should be together at Christmas.

Don't think like that – just get on with your work. Parents' Evening was looming and her mother, despite having a reputation as a fun-loving media person, was distinctly lacking in humour when it came to falling grades.

Perhaps a chocolate biscuit would help. Maybe she was suffering from low blood sugar.

She opened the bedroom door and stepped out on to the landing. From the sitting-room below drifted the strains of some American folk singer warbling *"How can I ever live without you?"*

She leaned over the bannister.

Her mum was slumped on the sofa, cradling a mug of coffee in her hands.

She was crying.

"Mum!" Chloë ran downstairs and put her arms round her mum. "Don't cry. Please!"

Her mum tried to smile. "I was just thinking about Dad . . ."

Chloë jumped up and switched off the stereo. "It won't do you any good listening to all that stuff," she said firmly.

Her mum sighed. "Don't you miss him too? Don't you want him to come home?"

Chloë stood looking at her mother.

She didn't know what to say.

Because she simply didn't know what she wanted to happen.

All she was absolutely certain of were those things she never wanted to happen again.

Chapter 5

ON THE RUN

"THANK YOU and do come again!" Josephine Johnson smiled politely to the last of the departing lunch-time customers and ran upstairs to the flat above the café, trilling a few notes of her favourite *Showboat* song as she did so. At last, she had a few minutes to herself; Jenny Bowen had agreed to come in for an hour or so to hold the fort. Harry was still in the kitchen, experimenting with recipes for what he assured her would be next month's Christmas rush and for once, she was happy to leave him there. She had to write a letter and she needed peace and quiet in which to do it.

She sat at the desk, kicked off her shoes and switched on the computer. Much as she worried about the money Harry had ploughed into the new café venture, she was thrilled with the new computer system. Gone were the days when she had to write to her sister Annie in Barbados; now all she did was type an e-mail, and the reply came whizzing back within hours.

Not that it was Annie she was writing to now; it was something far more exciting. And for now, very secret.

She logged on to the server and went into the new mail to check whether her sister had sent the Christmas present list for her kids.

And gasped out loud in horror at what appeared on the screen.

Hi, Sexy Lady!
Remember the wonderful time we had?
How we danced cheek to cheek at the disco? How you laughed at that weird movie? Remember the way we kissed?

What on earth . . . !

It couldn't be for them. Someone must have made a mistake.

But it was addressed to them – Johnson@cancaf.uk.

She scrolled through the message, gulping as she did so.

Well, I've got a surprise for you . . . do it all again soon . . . running my fingers . . .

Oh really! This was just too appalling. Josephine's heart pounded as she forced herself to read on.

". . . watch this space . . . miss you, babe!"

She flinched with distaste. Who on earth would send such a thing? She scrolled to the return address, a frown puckering her forehead as she struggled to make sense of it.

It meant nothing to her. It wasn't for her, that was for sure. And it certainly wasn't for Harry.

Which only left . . .

But it couldn't be.

It could.

She wouldn't.

She might.

No. Not Jasmin. Jasmin's so innocent.

Isn't she?

She had better be.

She peered at the screen once more.

Hang in there, babe! Till my lips meet yours, You Know Who!

Disgusting! It will be one of these new friends of hers, Josephine thought. They are leading her astray. All this dashing about town at all hours – she never used to be like that. Why couldn't she have stuck with Faith and Shelley, nice African-Caribbean girls with a sense of what was right and proper?

Keep calm. You don't know all the facts. Don't overreact. Wait until you have a chance to talk to her about it.

Just wait till she gets back.

I'll kill her.

———

Jasmin stood outside City Museum, wondering what to do next. She had been hanging around for nearly an hour now and she was freezing cold. Sanjay hadn't been there when she panted up to the entrance; not that she had really expected him to wait. She had looked round the museum in the hope of finding him, but she hadn't been able to get into the rooms set aside for the exhibition. That cost two pounds fifty and in her rush she had come out without her purse. So she had just paced up and down the street, looking at the Christmas windows in the shops and waiting for him to come out.

She glanced at the clock on the shop over the road. Three-thirty. He couldn't still be in there, surely? More likely he had got fed up and gone home before she got there. He was probably at his flat right now, thinking that she had stood him up, hating her for letting him down.

There and then, she made up her mind. She crossed the road and headed off down the street. She knew he lived at Avenue Mansions, although she had no idea which flat. But she could find out.

She glanced at the overcast sky and quickened her step. She was still pretty nervous being out on her own at the best of times, after what had happened to her dad, and she certainly wanted to be home before it began to get dark. It was easy to pretend to be brave when she was with her mates, but on her own the memories came flooding back.

But even her terror of the dark faded into the background compared with her fear at upsetting Sanjay.

She had never had a boyfriend before, and she was prepared to do whatever it took to keep him. He was kind and gentle and he never laughed at any of her hang-ups. And heaven knew, there were enough of them.

And unless she was very much mistaken, this was the easy part. If they really were going to be an item, there was another, far bigger problem looming just around the corner.

———

"That was great, wasn't it, Sanjay?"

Mr Buckley pulled his overcoat round him and shivered

as they stepped out into the dusk.

"Yes, sir," said Sanjay. Despite his disappointment over Jasmin, his mind was bursting with ideas from the exhibition and he wanted to dash home and put them into practice. "I do wish that I could . . ."

He stopped speaking in mid sentence.

"What?"

"I wish I could do that sort of stuff as a career," he said. "You know, 3-D films, teaching aids for kids. Silly, I know."

"Not silly at all!" enthused Mr Buckley, moving over to the bus stop and glancing down the street. "I thought that was where you were heading anyway."

"My dad wants me to do law," said Sanjay flatly.

"But it's not your father who is going to be doing it, is it?" reasoned Mr Buckley. "Surely he's proud of all the work you've produced so far?"

"He doesn't know about most of it," admitted Sanjay. "He's not really into that kind of stuff. He says that film and television are responsible for half the world's ills."

"Does he now?" his teacher replied dryly. "But, Sanjay, you have a real talent, one which must be nurtured. Oh look, here comes my bus!"

He moved forward to the kerb. "Look, you just leave it with me," he called over his shoulder. "I'll have a word with your father at Parents' Evening."

"No, sir!"

Mr Buckley looked astonished.

"I mean, it doesn't matter," mumbled Sanjay.

"Doesn't it, Sanjay?" mused Mr Buckley. "Doesn't it really?"

Right, Nick told himself firmly. That was it. From today, things were going to be different. It was time he got his act together, put the past behind him and concentrated on getting a life. And the first thing he had to do was ring Chloë and apologise for running off like that.

He stood up and walked purposefully over to the telephone kiosk.

The number rang and rang, but there was no answer.

Well, there wouldn't be. She was probably out with her mates having a good time.

If he hadn't messed up, she would be with him now, down at the ice rink, having a laugh.

Instead of which, she was probably out with Jasmin and Sinead, laughing about him.

He pushed open the kiosk door and broke into a jog.

Maybe he should forget about Chloë and relationships, which he was obviously useless at, and concentrate on something he could do.

Like sport.

Not that there was much chance of that at Lockbridge High. Not like Benham Grange.

Stop it. Don't look back.

Just stop thinking. And keep running.

———

"Don't answer it, Mum!" Chloë grabbed her mother's arm as she stretched out to pick up the telephone. "Just leave it."

"But, darling," reasoned Suzy, "it could be someone important."

"It will be Dad and you know it," retorted Chloë. "He's

phoned three times in the last two hours – and however much he pleads, I'm not going to change my mind."

Her mother sighed. "He is your father, sweetheart – and he's never done you any harm," she began. "Don't you think you should at least hear him out?"

"No!" There was a catch in Chloë's voice as she blinked back unshed tears. "I don't want to see him. And I don't want to talk to him. He scares me."

She hadn't meant to say that. In fact, she hadn't even realised that she felt that way.

She was being stupid. He was her own father, for heaven's sake. And he had never once laid a finger on her.

But it was true – she was frightened of him. Frightened of what he had done to her mother, frightened of what she was quite sure he was capable of doing again.

And yet at the same time, she loved him. Surely she shouldn't love a man like that? Sometimes she wished she was five years old again, riding on her dad's shoulders, blissfully unaware of what he could be like, believing that he was just the same as everyone else's dad.

"Look, Chloë love," began her mother, "you mustn't take against your father just because of what's happened between him and me."

Oh mustn't I? thought Chloë. What a perfectly stupid, meaningless thing to say.

"I'm going to finish my homework," she said, jumping up and heading for the stairs. "And whatever you do, don't answer the phone."

She had to be strong, she knew that. She had to be the logical, level-headed one, keeping her mum on an even keel.

But she didn't feel strong. She felt confused and angry and scared.

And very, very lonely.

———

If she didn't stop, she thought she would very probably die. Sinead leaned against a lamppost, clutching her side and gasping for breath. For someone who used any excuse she could think of to get out of games, a five-minute run in the teeth of what felt like a force nine gale had been a pretty stupid idea. Pointless, too. Her chances of bumping into Nick were rather lower than the chances of collapsing from overexertion.

She glanced wearily along the waterfront, wondering whether a large doughnut at The Canal Café wouldn't be infinitely preferable to running the remaining two blocks to the DIY store. She could have a gossip with Jasmin and she might even get a free cappuccino out of Mrs Johnson or Nick's mum, – always assuming it was her Sunday on duty, of course.

Nick's mum! That was it! She could drop Nick's name into the conversation, really casually, say she needed his help with her homework, and Nick's mum would say that was fine, and why didn't she pop round for supper tonight? It was brilliant.

She stopped to tighten the laces on her trainers and set off along the waterfront. It was beginning to get dark and she shivered, wishing she had put a jacket on over her sweatshirt.

And then she saw him. It was him, she knew it. He was some way off, but there was no mistaking that long, athletic stride and mass of flopping brown hair. And he was running straight towards her.

Oh my God. Look casual. Look as if he is the last person you expect to see.

She began running in what she hoped was the sort of slow motion, sexy way they did it in the adverts, running her fingers through her dark-blonde hair and praying that her nose hadn't turned red in the cold.

He was getting closer. She did hope her armpits weren't smelly with all the exertion.

Keep calm. Smile. Oh my God.

———

That girl looks familiar, thought Nick pounding along the canal path. Oh no. It can't be. It is. Sinead.

I can't face her now. She's bound to ask questions and I haven't worked out a good enough excuse yet.

She hasn't seen me.

Maybe if I pick up speed and keep my head down she won't notice me.

She's noticed me.

Sugar.

———

"Hi, Nick!" Sinead greeted him with what she hoped was a look of total surprise.

"Out for a run?"

It was a pretty dumb question but she was too short of breath to embark on intelligent conversation.

Nick nodded, pausing to run on the spot.

"Me too," she panted, wishing he would stand still for two seconds.

Nick looked surprised. "I didn't know you liked running," he said.

"Oh yes," Sinead replied nonchalantly, trying desperately to think of a way of changing the subject before Nick suggested a quick sprint over to Bradford. "Well, a lot more than I like French anyway. I am currently running away from my homework."

Nick burst out laughing. "You are funny!" he chuckled. "It will still be there when you get home."

"Tell be about it," sighed Sinead. "I don't suppose by any chance you're good at languages, are you?"

Nick shrugged. "Average," he said.

"Which is a big improvement on my efforts," Sinead replied. 'If Sinead were to be stranded in Paris, it is unlikely she would find her way to the nearest phone box, let alone manage to get home.' That's what Miss Finch said in my last report." Nick laughed again.

"Oh well, good luck with it," he said, turning to leave.

You can't go. Not yet. Not now.

"I don't suppose," she babbled, "that you could bear a quick coffee in The Canal Café and a squint at this?"

She waved her exercise book in his face. "Please? I'll pay."

Nick hesitated.

"Sorry," said Sinead, kicking herself for being so obvious. "I guess you're in a hurry."

Nick chewed his lip and took a deep breath. "OK," he said.

Sinead was speechless with delight.

"Look, about Friday," Nick began, staring ahead of him as they walked over to the café. "The thing is – well, actually what happened was . . ."

His voice tailed off and Sinead saw that he was staring intently at the pavement, his face diffused with colour.

"It's OK," she said easily. "It was no big deal."

For an instant, a look of hope crossed his face. "Yes, but – well, what did Chloë – what did the others say?"

Sinead knew what she wanted to say. Chloë was furious, Chloë never wants to speak to you again, so you might as well forget her and concentrate on me.

"Everyone was fine about it – we guessed what had happened."

Nick's eyes widened in alarm. "What do you mean, you guessed?"

Suddenly Sinead realised that whatever the real reason behind his behaviour, what she had to do was make him feel better.

"We've all done it," she said cheerfully, pushing open the door of the café and thinking on her feet. "Got to a restaurant and realised we had no money. It's so embarrassing."

Her inventiveness was rewarded by Nick's sigh of relief. "That's right," he said eagerly. "And then when I got home, I'd forgotten my key, and Mum was out so I . . ."

"Nick!"

"Yes?"

"Forget it, OK?" said Sinead. "Just apply your mind to things that matter."

"Like what?"

"Whether you want a cinnamon or a chocolate doughnut."

Nick threw back his head and laughed.

He really was, thought Sinead, quite unbelievably sexy.

———

She couldn't do it. Jasmin stood on the bridge overlooking the canal and willed herself to go on. Sanjay's apartment block was only a couple of streets away.

But it was getting dark. And there was a crowd of guys on the other side of the bridge, laughing and joking, and she would have to walk right past them.

It would be all right.

Nothing would happen.

They were just having a laugh and a joke. They wouldn't take any notice of her.

She took a couple of steps and stopped. In her mind all she could see was that gloomy London street, her father lying in a pool of blood on the pavement and the sound of guys laughing as they ran away.

At that moment, one of the boys on the bridge spun round and caught her eye.

She turned and ran as fast as she could along the waterfront and home.

———

"Sanjay? Is that you?"

No, it's Little Red Riding Hood, thought Sanjay viciously, slamming the front door and kicking off his trainers.

"Yeah," he grunted.

"And about time too!" exclaimed his father, sticking his head round the kitchen door. "I've just been into your room and it appears you still haven't finished your Mathematics homework!"

Sanjay bristled. How dare his dad go rummaging through his things?

"I'll do it later, it's no big deal," he murmured.

"Oh, no big deal, is it?" retorted his father. "And I suppose your GCSEs next summer are no big deal, either?"

Sanjay sighed. "I didn't say that," he began.

"You have to remember, Sanjay," his father continued, "that excellence is not achieved by half-hearted measures. It seems to me that lately you have been growing rather lackadaisical in your approach to work."

You mean, thought Sanjay, that lately I have actually had more exciting things to do than swot over books all weekend.

"I'll do it now," he said. "Oh, and by the way, did anyone phone while I was out?"

His father frowned and shook his head. "No one," he said. "Why, were you expecting a call?"

Sanjay sighed. "No," he said. "No, I wasn't expecting anything. Nothing at all."

Chapter 6

MOTHERS IN CRISIS

"LET'S SIT in the corner, OK?"

"Sure."

Nick would have happily sat on the roof if Sinead had suggested it, so great was his relief. She had said that Chloë was all right about Friday. As long as he stuck with that wicked story about forgetting his money, everything would be OK.

Sinead began leading the way to one of the high-backed booths at the far end of the café. Nick had just paused to drool quietly over the chill cabinet of cakes and pastries when the rear door was flung open and Mrs Johnson burst through, looking very fraught.

"Harry! Harr-eee!"

She caught sight of Nick and Sinead and stopped in her tracks.

"Oh, so you're back?"

Sinead and Nick looked up in surprise.

"Oh, hi, Mrs Johnson," Sinead replied. "Can we have two cappuccinos and . . ."

"Where's Jasmin?"

"Excuse me?" Sinead frowned.

"Jasmin – where is she? Nick?"

Nick coughed and glanced at Sinead, who shrugged her shoulders. "I – er, I don't know," he said, wondering what on earth she was on about.

Josephine frowned. "What do you mean, you don't know? You all came back together, surely?"

"Back from where?" Nick and Sinead spoke in unison.

Mrs Johnson's eyes narrowed and she put her hands on her ample hips. "Jasmin told me she was meeting you to go to some museum," she said. "Are you telling me you knew nothing about it?"

I'm keeping quiet, thought Nick. What I don't say I can't be blamed for.

"Oh, that wasn't us, Mrs Johnson," said Sinead politely. "Chloë told me – Sanjay was dragging her along to some computer animation exhibition . . ."

"Sanjay? Computer exhibition?" Mrs Johnson looked aghast.

"Yes," nodded Sinead. "He's the school computer whizz kid."

"Is he indeed?" muttered Mrs Johnson through gritted teeth. "That explains a lot."

Nick and Sinead exchanged puzzled glances.

"And she distinctly said she was meeting you!" she expostulated. "That does it! First that . . ." She gestured impatiently up the stairs. "And now lies! Just wait till I see Jasmin."

She stormed across the café to the kitchen. She had just

reached the door when she stopped dead and turned to Nick. "I don't suppose the words 'hang in there' and 'miss you, babe' mean anything to you?"

"Pardon?"

And to think that at Chloë's party she had seemed so normal.

"Oh forget it!" and with that Josephine crashed through the swing doors into the kitchen.

"What on earth . . .?" began Nick.

"Menopause," said Sinead knowledgeably. "They go doolally, it's a known fact. With mine, it's dusting."

Perhaps, thought Nick to himself, my mother is verging on the normal by comparison.

"Nick darling!" The swing doors lurched open once more and Jenny Bowen dashed through, balancing a tray of cutlery which she dumped on the table. "And Sinead? Well now, isn't this lovely, the two of you together like this? I'm so pleased!"

On the other hand, thought Nick, perhaps not.

"Mum!" He tried to inject a note of warning into his voice. "What are you doing here?"

Jenny smiled and brushed a stray strand of hair from her eyes. "Josephine was having a bit of a bad day . . ."

"I'd never have guessed," Sinead giggled.

"Pardon, dear?"

"Nothing."

"So I said I'd come in for an hour or so," Nick's mum continued. "You look better, Nick – Sinead been cheering you up, has she? That's nice. You see, I said if you got out with your friends . . ."

"Mum . . ."

"He gets a bit down sometimes, you know," she added, turning to Sinead.

"MUM!" How could she do that? Didn't she have any discretion? Luckily, Sinead appeared not to have noticed. "Can you just get us some coffees, please!"

Jenny beamed.

"And doughnuts?" Sinead pleaded, suddenly coming to life. "Cinnamon ones?"

"Leave it to me," said Jenny, winking at Nick before disappearing through the door.

Nick thought frantically of something to say. Anything to draw attention away from his embarrassing mother. "This French homework, then," he gabbled. "Chuck it over."

Sinead had just handed the book over when the bell on the café door jangled and Jasmin belted through, slamming it behind her.

"Hi, Jasmin! Over here!" Sinead beckoned frantically.

Jasmin stopped dead, catching her breath. "Oh, hi."

As she came reluctantly towards them, it was obvious that she had been crying.

"Are you OK?" Nick asked.

"Yes, fine." Jasmin gave a watery smile.

"Listen," said Sinead urgently, "I think we might have dropped you in it with your mum. You see, what happened was . . ."

"Jasmin! About time too!" Mrs Johnson strode into the room, her gold bangles jangling on her wrist. "Upstairs. Now."

"Mum!" Jasmin protested. "I'm talking to . . ."

"Now, Jasmin." She shoved Jasmin in the direction of the staircase just as Jenny appeared with the coffee and doughnuts.

"Oh, Jasmin, you're back!" she said. "Shall I get you something? Are you going to join the others?"

"No," retorted Josephine as they disappeared upstairs. "She is not."

Jenny pulled a face at Sinead and Nick. "Oh dear – trouble?"

Sinead nodded. "And actually," she said, biting her lip, "I think there's about to be some more."

"Why? What's wrong?"

Sinead looked apologetic. "I forgot my money. I can't pay."

Nick looked at Sinead and Sinead grinned back.

"And," said Nick. "So did I!"

They both burst out laughing.

"It's my treat," said Nick's mum, looking from one to the other in a rather puzzled manner.

"Thanks, Mrs Bowen," beamed Sinead. "Are you sure?"

"Oh yes," said Jenny. "Absolutely sure. It's so good to see Nick . . ."

"Mum!"

"I'll be getting on in the kitchen, then," said Jenny hastily.

"You do that, Mum," said Nick. "Now."

———

That would have to do. Chloë rammed the top on her pen and stuffed her English essay into her schoolbag. It was a pathetic attempt, but her brain was too scrambled to think of anything better. And if old Reilly didn't like it, it was just tough.

She was starving. After talking to her dad she had only managed to pick at her lunch and now her stomach was rumbling in protest. She clattered downstairs in the hope that her mum might be making a cake for tea.

She wasn't.

She was sitting on the floor, surrounded by photograph albums.

And she was crying again.

"Mum! What is it now?"

She hadn't meant it to come out like that, but she hated to see her mother so miserable all the time.

She jumped down the last two stairs and ran to put a comforting arm round her shoulders.

"I was just looking at all these pictures," Suzy sniffed. "Look – there's you with Dad at the zoo, do you remember? When you insisted that all you wanted for your fifth birthday was a giraffe?"

Chloë nodded.

"And look – here's one of you and Dad with that toboggan he made you! And look – this is when we went to Italy and . . ."

Chloë leaned over and slammed the album shut. "Mum, don't do this to yourself!" she said. "Think about something nice."

"Like what?"

Chloë chewed her lip. "Like your show being nominated for that award – what was it that paper called you? 'The best thing to happen at breakfast since microwaveable sausages!' "

Suzy tried a wan smile.

Chloë pressed on. "And talking of sausages, what's for supper?"

Suzy sighed and shrugged her shoulders. "I don't know," she said wearily. "I'm not that hungry."

"Well, I am!" asserted Chloë. "And besides, starving yourself won't help."

Honestly, sometimes her mother was worse than a child.

"Look, I'll cook my speciality, OK?"

Suzy jumped to her feet and held up her hands in mock surrender.

"No, no – anything but that," she laughed, wiping her eyes. "Your toasted peanut butter and cheese would be the final straw!"

Chloë grinned.

At least her mum was smiling again.

For now.

———

"Mum!" Jasmin wheeled round to face her mother as they reached the top of the stairs. "How could you do that in front of my friends?"

"Quite easily," retorted Josephine, opening the door to the office and waving Jasmin in. "Now sit down and listen to me."

She pushed Jasmin on to the swivel chair in front of the desk.

"I found an e-mail," hissed her mother. "An e-mail which started 'Hi, Sexy Lady.' " She spat out the words, wrinkling her nose in obvious distaste at the memory.

"What . . . ?" Jasmin looked puzzled.

"Now don't you try to pull the wool over *my* eyes, young lady!" retorted her mother. "What's all this about . . . ?"

She paused. "Kissing – and surprises and . . ."

She took a deep breath. "And the phrase, 'you sexy lady'!"

"Oh, wow!" Jasmin's face lit up as realisation dawned. "That's amazing. Oh, fantastic! He replied!"

"Oh, amazing, is it?" stormed her mother, glaring at Jasmin. "Well that tells me all I need to know!"

She ran her fingers distractedly through her hair.

"So where is it?" demanded Jasmin. "I want to read it."

"Oh, I'm quite sure you do," retorted her mother. "But you can't. I binned it. It's hardly the sort of stuff I want a child of mine to read!"

"But it's . . ."

"Let me tell you here and now that I am appalled. Horrified. And just who is this . . . this person that you have been consorting with? As if I didn't know!"

She stabbed at the computer with her finger, as if the machine was responsible for the whole thing.

"*Me?*" exclaimed Jasmin. "It's nothing to do with me!"

Her mother sniffed, thrust out her ample bosom and folded her arms. "Come on, Jasmin, I wasn't born yesterday! It's nothing to do with me or with your father, Flora and Tom are away at uni – there's only you left."

"Yes, but . . ."

"And don't you try telling me another whole load of lies," snorted Josephine. "Telling me that you were going to a museum with your friends when all the time . . ."

"I did go!" retorted Jasmin furiously.

"Don't lie to me! Nick and Sinead told me they hadn't seen you . . ."

Jasmin stamped her foot in frustration. "I do have other friends, you know!" she shouted.

"Oh yes – Sanjay Fraser, for example. And don't try lying your way out of that one," she warned, as Jasmin opened her mouth. "I suppose he sent you this rubbish!"

Jasmin looked horrified. "Sanjay? Of course he didn't! I keep telling you!"

"So, just what have you two really been doing all afternoon?"

"Nothing – thanks to you!" shouted Jasmin. "We were going to the exhibition at the City Museum, but he didn't wait because I was late. And I was late because *you* kept finding jobs for me to do!"

For a moment her mother had the good grace to look mildly apologetic. The moment didn't last long.

"So how do I know the message wasn't from him? That sort of language – I can't believe that after all that your father and I have done . . ."

"Mum! Will you just shut up and listen! Of course it wasn't Sanjay – it didn't have his address on, did it?"

Jasmin, hands on hips, glared at her mother.

"How should I know?" said her mother, looking slightly confused. "It was some incomprehensible jargon – ski something, with GR at the end."

"There you are, then!" cried Jasmin triumphantly. "Told you!"

Her mother frowned. "Told me what?"

"That e-mail was for Chloë, not me!"

"Chloë? Chloë Sanderson?" Mrs Johnson slumped down on to a chair.

Jasmin nodded. "She met this guy on holiday and he promised to write, but he didn't, and she phoned but she couldn't get hold of him, so I suggested that she should e-mail him, but her parents don't have e-mail so I said I'd do it. OK?"

Her mother's eyes narrowed. "Are you telling me the truth?"

"Yes! And if you must know, that's how we got Chloë's mum to do the café opening – Chloë agreed to ask her in exchange for me sending the e-mail."

"Oh, did she now!" Mrs Johnson surveyed her fingernails for a moment. "Well, that just goes to show what low standards these white girls have!"

"Mum!"

"I'm sorry, but I have to say my piece. If you had read that thing . . ."

"You didn't give me the chance," stressed Jasmin. "So what did it say?"

"If you think I'm going to repeat all that filth," began her mother. "All I will say is that I'm quite sure that Suzy Sanderson would be horrified if she knew what was going on. She seems such a decent sort of woman."

"Decent enough to let her daughter have a life!" hissed Jasmin. "Her mum doesn't throw a fit every time she goes out with a boy!"

Her mother wrung her hands and sighed. "Darling," she said more gently, "it's not that I object to you having friends – even friends who are boys – provided that they are, well – suitable."

"Oh, and Sanjay's not?"

"Jasmin, we've been through this before. I have no doubt that Sanjay is a nice enough boy, and he seems very polite, but he's not . . ."

"Not what? Black? Go on, say it!"

Her mother said nothing.

"You are unbelievable, you know that?" stormed Jasmin. "How can you be so prejudiced?"

"I just think," ventured her mother, "that you should see more of your African-Caribbean friends. Shelley and Faith – now Faith's brother, what's he called? Tony! He's a lovely lad."

"He," said Jasmin, "is a dweeb. Now do you very much mind if I go back downstairs and talk to my friends?"

"Very well," sighed Josephine. "And Jasmin?"

"What?"

"In future, you will not use this computer without my consent. In fact, you will not come into the office, do you understand?"

"Oh terrific!" snapped Jasmin. "Lock me in my bedroom and throw away the key, why don't you? After all, you don't want me to have any sort of a life!"

Josephine sighed. "It's not like that," she said. "I do have your best interests at heart, darling, believe me. I just understand more about the world than you do."

"Oh yeah?" Jasmin threw her a poisonous glance and stomped downstairs and into the café.

Jenny was wiping the now empty table.

"Oh, hello dear," she beamed. "Nick and Sinead have just left."

"Now look what you've done!" Jasmin spun round and glared at her mother who was close on her heels. "You've trashed Chloë's mail, you've laid into me for something that wasn't my fault and you've made me look a complete jerk in front of my mates! Well I hope that you are satisfied!"

Jenny and Josephine exchanged glances.

"Now you're getting things out of all proportion," protested Josephine with a sigh.

"Oh, am I?" retorted Jasmin. "And I wonder where I get that from?"

———

"I didn't handle that very well, did I?"

Jasmin's mum looked anxiously at Jenny Bowen, who was arranging flowers on the tables in readiness for the evening rush.

Jenny smiled. "Show me a parent who can handle their teenager and I'll show you a miracle worker," she said, snipping the end of a freesia stem. "I'm always putting my foot in it with Nick."

Josephine sighed and began folding table napkins. "Yes, but boys are so much easier than girls, aren't they?" she said. "None of those rampant emotions to deal with. Count yourself lucky."

"Oh, yes, it's a bundle of laughs!" sighed Jenny, putting the glass vase on the table with rather more force than was necessary. "Being a single mum, putting up with the long silences, the sullen stares, the anger and the grief he can't, or won't express about his father . . . sometimes I feel I just can't cope." Her voice cracked.

"Oh, Jenny, I'm so sorry!" Josephine dropped the napkins and put an arm round Jenny's shoulder. "I didn't think."

"It's OK," Jenny sniffed. "It's just all getting on top of me – living with Mum, scrimping and saving for a deposit, missing Greg . . ."

She sank down on to a chair and buried her face in her hands.

"My dear, how thoughtless of me!" murmured Josephine. "Here's me, so caught up with worrying about Jasmin and planning my own escape and . . ." Her voice trailed away and she suddenly became very preoccupied with her table napkins.

Jenny wiped her eyes and looked at her curiously. "Escape? Surely you and Harry can't be thinking of . . . ?"

The swing doors crashed open and a smell of cardamon and cinnamon wafted through to the café.

"Harry can't be thinking of what?" Mr Johnson looked enquiringly at Jenny. Josephine pulled a face at her and frantically shook her head.

"Oh, er – closing for Christmas," replied Jenny, latching on to the first thought that came into her mind.

"No way!" exclaimed Harry, rubbing his hands enthusiastically. "In fact, I've been thinking about that idea of yours, Jenny. And I guess it's a winner."

"What idea?" asked Josephine.

"A great three-day extravaganza – Caribbean Christmas Canalside! Steel bands, limbo dancing, the works!"

"And that was your idea?" asked Josephine, turning to Jenny.

She nodded.

"Oh terrific," sighed Josephine.

———

Jasmin dialled Sanjay's number and waited, biting her lip, as the number rang.

"Hello!"

"Oh, hi, this is Jasmin Johnson – may I speak to Sanjay?"

"No, you can't."

Jasmin gulped. "Oh, is he out?"

"No, he's not."

Jasmin frowned and tried again. "Is that Mrs Fraser?"

"No, it's me. You can talk to me, though, if you like."

Jasmin was getting very irritated. "And who are you?"

"Rani. Sanjay's sister."

Jasmin vaguely remembered that Sanjay had mentioned that he had a younger sister. He hadn't said she was the most awkward child on earth.

"Jasmin!" Her mother was calling from the kitchen, and her voice did not suggest that she was in the most charming of moods. "Will you get off that telephone this instant and come here?"

Jasmin dropped her voice and hissed down the phone. "I don't want to speak to you. I want to speak to Sanjay. So will you please go and get him."

"No!"

There was a click and the line went dead.

"Well, thank you for nothing!" Jasmin slammed the phone down. Wretched child – how dare she? Unless . . .

That was it. Rani was probably only doing what she had been told to do.

Sanjay had obviously made it quite clear to his entire family that on no account did he want to speak to Jasmin Johnson ever again.

Chapter 7

HIGH HOPES,
DASHED HOPES

CHLOË ROLLED over in bed and slammed her hand on the shrilling alarm. She had only just pulled the duvet over her head and closed her eyes again, when another clock clanged on the landing, swiftly followed by a third balanced high on the top of the wardrobe.

"All right, all right, I get the message!" muttered Chloë, throwing back the duvet and stomping over to the other side of the bedroom. The clocks were her mother's idea; now that she was presenting 'The Breakfast Break' on Pennine TV she had to leave the flat at five o'clock every morning and didn't trust Chloë to make it to school on time.

Not that she was in the mood for school. She knew that essay was the pits and those Maths equations – oh no! Maths! She had completely forgotten to do it. Old Tommo would go ballistic. Perhaps she could phone in sick and do it today.

Actually, that was a pretty cool idea.

Come to think of it, she could almost feel a headache coming on.

As if picking up her thoughts by telepathy, her mother's face loomed up on the portable TV on Chloë's chest of drawers. That was another of her mother's little ploys, setting the television to come on at just the moment she thought Chloë would be falling asleep again.

Chloë paused and gazed at the screen where her mother was engaged in animated conversation with two extraordinarily dressed women who apparently believed they were housing aliens in their garden shed. Suzy was smiling and gesturing, looking as if she could think of no more fascinating way to spend the morning. And tonight, thought Chloë with a sigh, as her mother's face faded to be replaced by an advert for uplift bras, you'll be in a heap on the sitting-room sofa again.

She had just clicked the TV off, and was padding along the landing to the bathroom when the telephone rang.

Here we go, thought Chloë with a wry grin, grabbing the extension from the table by her mother's bed.

"Yes, I'm up, no, I won't forget to lock the door and yes, I will eat breakfast," she chanted, knowing full well that her mum would be using the advert break to check up on her and not being prepared to let on that she didn't intend to budge one inch.

"There's a good girl!" There was a burst of giggles at the other end of the telephone. "It's me, you idiot – Jasmin!"

"Oh, sorry, I thought you were my mum."

"I gathered," replied Jasmin. "Listen, you'll never guess what's happened!"

"You and Sanjay fell madly in love while gazing at a glass case in the museum," suggested Chloë with a chuckle.

"That's not remotely funny!"

Jasmin's retort took Chloë by surprise.

"Sorry!"

"It's OK," said Jasmin. "I'll explain later."

"So what has happened, then?" coaxed Chloë.

"It came!"

"Pardon?"

"The e-mail, silly – it arrived!"

Chloë almost dropped the telephone in her surprise. "What? From him? Jack? To me?"

"No, from the man in the moon to the Queen of Sheba – of course, from Jack. How many other people have you been e-mailing?"

"Oh my God! Oh, that's so brilliant! I can't believe it! What does he say?"

There was a slight pause. "Well, that's the thing . . ." Jasmin began.

Chloë could hear the slamming of a door down the phone and raised voices in the background.

"What do you mean, that's the thing?" she demanded.

"Hang on," hissed Jasmin. "Mother on the warpath. I'll explain later."

Chloë nodded, abandoning all ideas of taking a sickie, and then realised that Jasmin couldn't see her. "All right, I'll meet you at the bus stop."

"OK," said Jasmin. "And Chloë?"

"Yes?"

"Don't forget to lock the door, there's a good girl!"

———

Sanjay strapped his schoolbag to the back of his bicycle and headed off up the road. Recently he had been taking the bus to school, because that way he got to talk to Jasmin, but today he was concentrating all his efforts on not seeing her. He knew that she would try to be nice and pretend that she had been ill or that her watch had stopped or something; he also knew that guys who were well hard didn't let on when they were upset. Only he wasn't too sure that if he came face to face with her he could keep his feelings to himself. So he would just keep well out of her way.

He yawned as he swerved off the cycle path. He had sat up late into the night, reading this cool book he had bought at the exhibition, all about 3-D computer animation. The trouble was, every time he started doodling a new idea for a cartoon character, he found himself writing the word *Jasmin* over and over again until he had filled half a pad of paper with her name and little sketches of her face. Dumb or what?

Perhaps his dad was right after all. Maybe he should just concentrate on studying and forget relationships. He'd done it for years; he had been stupid to expect that anything would ever change.

As he drew up to the traffic-lights they changed to red. As he braked, he saw Jasmin. She was talking to Chloë Sanderson, and instinctively he opened his mouth to call her name. And closed it again.

She wouldn't want to talk to him. If she had, she would have phoned and explained what had happened. The fact that he hadn't heard a word told him all he needed to know.

"Come on, come on, give it to me!" Chloë hopped up and down from one foot to the other in her excitement.

Jasmin took a deep breath. "I haven't got it," she said.

For a moment, Chloë's face fell and then she brightened. "So we can print it out later," she said, as the bus pulled up at the stop. "The thing is, what did he say?"

Jasmin bit her lip. "Well – he called you a sexy lady," she began, climbing on to the bus and rather hoping that they would get separated.

They didn't.

"Really? He said that? He called me sexy?"

Chloë hurled her schoolbag on to the overhead rack and gazed at Jasmin in open-mouthed delight.

Jasmin nodded, her eyes scanning the bus to see where Sanjay was sitting.

She couldn't see him anywhere.

"Well, go on – what else did he say?" urged Chloë.

"There was something about kissing. I think." Jasmin faltered, grabbing the handrail as the bus pulled away.

"He has lips to die for," Chloë swooned. "Oh, Jasmin, do get on with it; just tell me what else he said!"

Jasmin sighed. "I don't know," she murmured. "I never got to read it."

"But you just said . . ."

"My mum deleted it from the system," confessed Jasmin.

"Your *mum*?" Chloë exclaimed. "*Deleted* it?"

Jasmin nodded miserably.

"And what exactly was your mother doing reading *my*

e-mail, for heaven's sake?"

Jasmin told her the whole story, pausing now and again while Chloë ranted and raved and got more and more annoyed. "And now she won't let me in the office again – she's even locked the door," she finished lamely. "Sorry."

"Sorry! Sorry! I should jolly well hope you are!"

Jasmin pulled back in amazement. "Hang on!" she retorted. "Don't blame me! My mother messed up – it's not my fault!"

"Yes it is!" snapped Chloë. "If you'd done what you promised, and checked the computer first thing every morning, this wouldn't have happened!"

"Oh great!" retaliated Jasmin. "It was my idea to send the e-mail in the first place, just because you were too dippy to make an overseas phonecall without having your hand held! So don't have a go at me!"

She jumped up, grabbed her bag as the bus pulled into the school forecourt and glanced out of the window. At the far side of the yard Sanjay was parking his bicycle. Her heart lurched.

"Sorry," muttered Chloë. "But you don't understand what it's like . . ."

"Oh yes I do!" retorted Jasmin, pushing her way to the front of the bus. "You're not the only person in the world with problems, you know! You're not the only one with feelings!"

Chloë opened her mouth but Jasmin was in full flood.

"At least you know that Jack cares! Just be grateful for that!"

Jasmin jumped off the bus and began running across the

forecourt, dodging in and out of the clusters of kids heading for the main door. Behind her, she could hear Chloë calling her name, but she ignored her.

All she wanted to do was catch up with Sanjay and make him understand.

"Jasmin, wait for me!" She heard footsteps pounding behind and turned, expecting to see Chloë on her heels.

It was Faith Carmichael, the girl she had been friendly with when she first moved up from London.

"Oh hi, Faith," Jasmin muttered, not slowing her pace.

"Slow down," panted Faith. "I need your help – it's my English homework. If I get another D-grade, my dad will go ballistic. Give me a hand before registration. Please!"

Jasmin craned her neck. Sanjay had unloaded his books from his bike and was heading in the direction of the computer room.

"Can't stop right now, Faith," she gabbled. "I'm in a tearing hurry."

"To do what?" demanded Faith. "Suck up to your oh-so-snooty white friends again? To hang around that geeky boy?"

"That's a horrible thing to say!"

"True, though – you never have any time for Shelley or me these days."

"It's not like that," began Jasmin. Sanjay rounded the corner of the main building and disappeared out of sight. "I've got to dash – I'll do it later."

"Don't bother!" yelled Faith. "Who needs you?"

Not Sanjay, that's for sure, thought Jasmin miserably.

And Chloë probably won't ever speak to me again.

And it's all my mother's fault.

———

He wouldn't have e-mailed at all if he didn't still care for me, thought Chloë, unloading school books into her locker. So he must be keen.

"Hi there!"

She turned to see Nick smiling at her.

"Oh, hi!"

But what did he say? How romantic was it? Does he want me to fly out for Christmas?

"Good weekend?"

Nick was eyeing her eagerly. She shrugged. "OK," she said.

Until my friend's mother messed up big-time.

Hang on – if Mrs Johnson read the e-mail, she must remember what it said.

"Look, I'm sorry about what happened on Friday . . ." Nick was still hovering at her left elbow.

That was it! Mega brill! Sorted!

"Sorry," she said, shaking herself out of her reverie. "What did you say?"

"I'm sorry about dashing off like that," Nick said.

Chloë remembered that Sanjay had said they should all make like it was of no importance.

"Friday? Oh, don't worry about it," she replied airily. "It didn't matter at all."

Nick's forehead puckered into a slight frown.

"Really? I mean, I didn't mean to spoil the evening."

"You didn't," Chloë said decisively. "No one gave it a second thought. Must dash. See you."

Had she not been so eager to tell Jasmin of her latest plan, she would have seen Nick staring after her with a look of intense disappointment on his face.

Chloë didn't see Jasmin until break-time and when she did finally catch up with her, Jasmin didn't seem overjoyed to see her.

"I've had this mega idea," Chloë began.

"How nice for you," mumbled Jasmin. "Have you seen Sanjay?"

"No," said Chloë. "Now listen. If your mum read the e-mail, she must remember what's in it. So this is what we do."

"We?" Jasmin raised an eyebrow.

"I come back to the café with you after school, and we ask your mum to repeat it word for word."

"I don't think that's a very good idea," began Jasmin.

"Look!" exploded Chloë. "Are you my friend or aren't you?"

"You tell me," shrugged Jasmin. "You didn't exactly sound friendly on the bus."

Chloë blushed and looked at Jasmin pleadingly. "I'm sorry," she said. "I was just upset. I know it's not your fault. It's your mum's. So we confront her."

"You don't know my mother," warned Jasmin, with a flicker of a smile. "She went on for ages about how a nice girl like you shouldn't be behaving in such a wayward manner."

Chloë waved a hand airily. "Oh don't worry about it," she said confidently. "I'll just do the mega-polite, how-are-you-Mrs-Johnson? bit and she'll be putty in my hands."

Jasmin looked doubtful but said nothing.

"So I can come? After school?"

"Sure," said Jasmin. "As long as you do all the talking."

"I will," said Chloë, giving her arm a friendly squeeze. "By the way, how did it go with Sanjay?"

Jasmin's face fell. "It didn't," she sighed.

"How come?"

Jasmin told her the whole story.

"And he won't speak to me when I phone, and he's avoiding me today . . ."

"It seems," said Chloë, "that your mother has a lot to answer for."

"Tell me about it," nodded Jasmin. "She's ruined everything."

"Don't let her," said Chloë decisively. "Confront Sanjay – say it how it is. Be assertive. That's what I'm going to do with your mother."

"That," said Jasmin, "is what worries me."

———

"Sanjay, wait!" Jasmin sped down the stairs after Sanjay, not caring that she would be late for Chemistry. "I have to talk to you."

Sanjay turned. "Hi," he said, inspecting something on the far wall with great concentration.

"About Sunday," she began. "I'm really sorry I didn't get there on time. My mum kept finding things for me to do."

"It's OK," Sanjay replied, stepping aside to let a clutch of Year Eights push past. "You don't have to pretend."

"What do you mean, pretend?" retorted Jasmin. "It's true. I got there twenty minutes late and there was no sign of you."

Sanjay didn't look convinced. "So why didn't you come inside and find me?"

"I did – well, the free part, anyway. I didn't have any cash on me for the exhibition."

Sanjay's face lightened and he almost smiled. "I thought you might phone . . ." he began.

"I did!" retorted Jasmin. "Only your dumb sister said I couldn't talk to you!"

"Don't you DARE!" Sanjay shouted. "Don't you ever speak about my sister like that!"

Jasmin drew back in amazement. "Sorry, I . . ."

"No, I'm sorry. It's just that Rani loves the telephone and she's getting quite good on it – but she's always naughty about telling us when there's a call, because she wants to do all the talking."

Jasmin frowned. This Rani sounded like one spoiled kid.

"So you hadn't told her to get rid of me?" Jasmin queried.

Sanjay looked astonished. "Of course not," he said. "I was desperate to talk to you."

The words were out before he could stop himself.

"Me too," said Jasmin. "I did try to come to your flat to find you but it was getting dark and there were these guys . . . I know it's stupid."

"No, it's not." Sanjay touched her hand briefly then snatched his away again. Little sparks of electricity shot through Jasmin's body.

"You actually tried that – to see me?" He seemed astounded.

Jasmin nodded.

"So," Sanjay began, "do you want – I mean, could we

try – or perhaps you don't . . ."

"Sanjay, I love you."

She couldn't believe she just said that. Girls weren't meant to be forward. That's what her mum always said. She'd be labelled easy, a tart. Or worse.

Sanjay gulped and stared at her.

She'd blown it. She knew she had.

The bell rang for the next lesson. Neither of them moved.

Sanjay coughed. "Well, the thing is," he began.

"Look, I'm sorry, OK?" gabbled Jasmin. "I shouldn't have . . ."

"The thing is," said Sanjay. "I think that actually, well, you know, that I love you too."

He touched her hand again. And this time he didn't let go.

———

"That is *so* romantic!" sighed Sinead over lunch after Jasmin had told her that she was deliriously and irrevocably in love. "You are lucky."

Jasmin grinned. "Still pining after Nick, are you?" she teased, biting into a cheese roll.

"No! Well, a bit. Not that there is any point."

Jasmin frowned. "Why not? You have to confront, be assertive," she added knowledgeably.

Sinead pulled a face. "All the assertiveness in the universe won't stop Nick fancying Chloë," she sighed. "I don't stand a chance."

Jasmin shrugged. "Well, Nick doesn't stand much of a chance either, does he?" she said. "All Chloë ever thinks about is this Jack guy."

Sinead pulled the ring off her can of lemonade. "Oh, that

was just a holiday romance," she said impatiently, taking a swig of drink. "She'll be all over Nick as soon as she realises Jack is never going to get in touch."

"He has," said Jasmin, peeling the lid off a pot of yoghurt.

Sinead spluttered, shooting a spray of lemonade all over the table. "What?"

Jasmin dropped her voice. "I don't think I'm supposed to say," she began, noticing with amusement how ecstatically happy Sinead looked all of a sudden, "but this is what happened . . ."

———

"Look, I really want to explain to you about Rani," said Sanjay during afternoon break. "It's just that I'm kind of protective towards her."

Jasmin looked puzzled.

"She doesn't do these things just to be awkward, you know," said Sanjay. "My sister has Down's syndrome."

Jasmin gasped. "Oh, Sanjay, I'm sorry, I really am," she exclaimed. "I didn't know."

"It's OK," said Sanjay with a smile.

"And besides, she doesn't sound mental."

His smile faded. "She's not mental, Jasmin," he retorted. "She has a learning disability. She's slower than you or me, that's all."

Jasmin bit her lip. "Sorry," she said again. "I just don't know anyone who is – well, you know . . ."

"She's really sweet," Sanjay told her. "Funny and affectionate – you'll love her when you meet her."

Jasmin gulped and said nothing.

For now, there was no need.

Chapter 8

DREAM ON!

WHILE HER daughter was spilling the beans at school, Josephine Johnson was rummaging through the racks of suits in Harvey Nichols, singing softly and wondering why the only outfits she liked were the ones she couldn't afford. Of course, if Harry knew what she was doing he would say that she didn't need anything new, that she had a wardrobe full of clothes. But then Harry didn't know about the audition.

She couldn't believe that they had replied so swiftly to her e-mail. Of course, she was probably wasting her time; there was no way they were going to take her. After all, it was months since she had sung regularly; with the café to run she had not even had time to join a church choir, let alone any spare evenings in the week for operatic societies or music groups. But she had to give it her best shot – she missed it all so much and the thought of spending the rest of her life laying tables and pouring wine and making small talk with customers was more than she could stand.

She grabbed a couple of outfits and headed for the changing cubicles. Harry would have to know sooner or later, and preferably before the Barclaycard bill landed on the mat.

But she wouldn't think about that right now. For now she would concentrate on more important things, like whether burgundy silk with a feather trim was really quite her style.

———

Dipti Fraser hugged the envelope close to her chest. She'd done it – it was ready to go! She felt more excited about this than any piece of work she had ever undertaken, so excited, in fact, that she was finding it very difficult not to tell her husband or Sanjay what she was doing. Sanjay would think she had flipped; he was such a sensible, studious boy, and as for Duncan, she could well imagine his reaction.

"Frivolous, meaningless nonsense!" he would declare in that patronising manner of his. "You can't be serious!"

That was one of his favourite phrases. But she was fed up with being serious, weary with writing learned volumes about Hindu mythology and culture and holding forth about Indian issues at seminars filled with stuffy academics.

There was nothing stuffy about this, she thought with a wry grin as she stuck stamps on the envelope and grabbed her coat from the hook behind the front door. In fact, parts of it were really rather naughty.

Which was why the name Dipti Fraser didn't appear anywhere on her manuscript. She rather liked being Venetia Valentine. She sounded like a woman who could have a whole secret life all of her own.

———

"And remember, breakfast isn't breakfast without 'The Breakfast Break'!"

Suzy held her smile until the producer waved his arm.

"Great, Suzy – thanks a bunch! Best programme trail we've recorded in ages!"

Suzy threw him one last glittering smile and then let her face relax. Thank heavens that was over; a three-hour breakfast show, a production meeting and then a recording session would have been tiring enough at the best of times, but after four weeks of broken nights and no appetite, she felt like a wreck.

"Great news about the show being nominated for the Best Magazine Show award, isn't it?" Nathan Reed, the producer, beamed and flopped down on to the chair next to her. "I bet Edward's tickled pink, isn't he? I know he loves these glamorous occasions."

Suzy's stomach lurched but she fixed a smile on her face and opened her mouth to say something suitably non-committal. The words wouldn't come.

"How is Ed, by the way?" Nathan continued eyeing her closely. "Pity that last series of his flopped – got something new up his sleeve, has he?"

Suzy took a deep breath and stood up. She had to get away.

"He's away at the moment," she said casually, gathering up her scripts. "Researching."

Nathan nodded slowly. "Oh well, I look forward to seeing him at the award ceremony," he smiled. "He's always good for a laugh!"

Suzy turned, snatched up her jacket from the back of the chair and headed for the door. "Must dash," she said, swallowing hard and willing herself to stay calm.

"Hang on!" Nathan called. "You've left your bag."

Reluctantly she turned, furiously blinking back the tears that had welled up at the thought of Edward.

"Suzy!" Nathan exclaimed. "What on earth is wrong? What is it, my dear?"

"Nothing," she said. "I'm fine. Absolutely fine."

And burst into tears.

———

Jenny Bowen stared forlornly in the window of Baxter and Bordiss, Estate Agents. It was hopeless; there was no way she could afford even a deposit on most of these places, and even if she did find the money, there was little chance of getting a mortgage on what she earned at the café.

And now Josie was talking about making her escape. She did hope that didn't mean they were going to sell up and go back to London. She loved The Canal Café; chatting to the customers and helping Harry to think up new money-spinning ideas took her mind off all the awful things that had happened and got her away from her mother. Not that her mum hadn't been great, taking her and Nick on and giving them a roof over their heads. But she was elderly and set in her ways and more than a little bit bossy; she drove Nick up the wall and when Nick was at odds with the world, they all suffered. It wasn't his fault, poor kid, she thought, turning away from the window and heading down Millers Lane towards the café; she felt so guilty, taking him away from boarding school and expecting him to settle somewhere new in his GCSE year. But what choice had she had? What choice had Nick's father left any of them?

If only she could find them a place of their own, somewhere

he could bring his friends without feeling embarrassed. Maybe she would call in on the estate agents later; perhaps they had some cheaper properties on their books.

She knew she was kidding herself. Short of winning the Lottery, they would be stuck at thirty-three Talbot Street for months yet.

"Don't you walk all over the carpet with those shoes!" Kathleen Flaherty grabbed her husband's arm and led him back to the doormat.

"Sorry, sorry!" Shaun kicked off his shoes and suppressed a sigh. "I'm not stopping, I've just popped back to collect the joint account cheque book."

"And want do you want that for?" demanded his wife. "Haven't you been spending enough lately?"

"Oh now, love," said her husband gently. "Don't be like that – we've got plenty these days, why not spend it?"

"Because," retorted Kathleen, "if you carry on frittering it away, it will all be gone and then where will we be? Back where we started from – not that that would be such a bad thing."

Shaun sighed. "Now what do you mean by that?" he asked, walking through to the kitchen and pulling open a drawer. "Are you telling me you'd rather be back in that draughty council house than living here in all this luxury?"

"At least at Burnthedge I knew people," Kathleen sighed. "I could have a gossip with the neighbours, and there was the church and . . ."

"There are churches round here," reasoned Shaun, slipping the cheque book into his jacket pocket. "I thought you'd been going to St Mary's."

Kathleen sniffed. "If you call that modern monstrosity a church," she said. "Father Ryan's young enough to be my son. And besides, I miss my garden."

Shaun threw back his head and laughed. "You make it sound as if we had rolling acres," he chuckled. "Instead of a balding lawn and a few wilting rose bushes."

"Well, it was something to do, wasn't it?" she replied with a catch in her voice. "Which is more than can be said for this place."

Shaun eyed his wife's flushed cheeks anxiously. "But, love," he said, slipping an arm round her shoulders, "there's the health club . . ."

"Oh yes, I'm really likely to appear there in my cossie, aren't I?" she said. "All thirteen stone of me."

"And there's the Sandersons upstairs," persisted Shaun. "You could get more friendly with Suzy."

"Do you really think a media star like her is going to be bothered with someone like me?" answered Kathleen.

She grabbed a cloth from the side of the kitchen sink and began wiping the counter tops as if her life depended on it.

Shaun glanced at his watch. "I must go, love," he said reluctantly. "I need to get to the bank."

Kathleen opened her mouth and then closed it again. "You go," she said. "I'll be fine."

Which, she thought as the front door closed behind her husband, is more than you will be when you get to Barclays and discover what I've done.

For the first time that day, a smile spread over her face and she began polishing the front of the fridge.

Chapter 9

A STEP FORWARD?

"I COULD come round this evening," Sanjay ventured to Jasmin at the end of afternoon school. "If you like."

"No!" Jasmin rejoined hastily.

"I see," sighed Sanjay, slamming shut the door of his locker.

"No you don't," said Jasmin. "I'd love you to come but . . ."

She faltered. She didn't know how to put it. If she told him the truth, he'd be really hurt and she couldn't bear that.

"Chloë's coming back with me," she said.

Sanjay frowned.

"I could make it later on," he suggested.

Jasmin sighed.

"My mum's a bit funny – about me and boys," she said lamely.

Sanjay frowned. "Well, she's going to have to know some time," he pointed out. "Besides, it's not as if she's never met me."

That, thought Jasmin, is part of the problem.

"Oh – you know what parents are like," she said airily,

hitching her schoolbag on her shoulder. "Weekdays are for homework, GCSEs matter more than fun, all that stuff."

"Tell me about it," nodded Sanjay. "OK – but I can phone you, can't I?"

Jasmin nodded eagerly. "Of course you can," she said.

Even her mother didn't bother to vet every phonecall.

Yet.

———

"I do not appear to have received your Maths homework, Chloë!" Mr Tompkins accosted her as she was pushing her way through the double doors into the playground with Nick. "Is there some valid explanation?"

Chloë put on her sweetest smile. "I'm sorry, sir," she said meekly. "I left it at home by mistake. I'll bring it in tomorrow."

"You do that, Miss Sanderson," he replied, "or we shall have to see whether detention sharpens your memory for you."

Chloë pulled a face behind his retreating back.

"Right bundle of laughs, isn't he?" said Nick, as they crossed to the rank of waiting buses.

"I reckon he's had a total charisma bypass," agreed Chloë, zipping up her jacket and shivering in the cold wind. "Terminal, I think."

Nick laughed. "Actually, I was thinking -- I don't suppose you fancy coming in to town for a bit? I can run to a couple of colas and double fries."

"I can't," Chloë replied, waving to Jasmin and Sinead, who were hopping up and down and beckoning to her. "I'm going home with Jasmin."

"Another time then," murmured Nick, trying not to sound disappointed.

"Sinead might go, or Sanjay," Chloë offered, remembering how they had all decided that Nick needed cheering up.

She was prevented from noting his lack of enthusiasm by Sinead, who dashed up to her and grabbed her arm. "At last!" she said. "I've been looking for you everywhere."

"Old Tommo was wittering on," said Chloë. "What did you want me for?"

"It's not me that wants you," she replied. "It's your dad."

"Dad!" Chloë gasped involuntarily as Sinead pointed across the school yard.

"He's over there," Sinead said. "He says he's come to give you a lift home."

———

She wouldn't go with him. How dare he turn up unannounced in front of all her friends?

Chloë glanced across the carpark. Her dad was striding towards her, a broad grin on his face.

She would have to go. Her mates all thought he'd been away on business – it would look pretty odd if she had a scene with him right now.

"I'd better go," she said with what she hoped was a long-suffering expression. "I'm sorry, Jasmin – I'll come tomorrow."

"No rush," said Jasmin with what appeared to be a certain amount of relief. "Say hi to your dad for me."

I will be saying more than that, thought Chloë. Considerably more.

"What are you doing here?" Chloë hissed as her father manoeuvred his BMW through the school gates. "I thought I told you I never wanted to see you again."

Her father turned to face her. "But you didn't mean that, did you, darling?" His voice was soft and gentle, his face grey and lined. "Please tell me you didn't really mean that."

No. Yes. I don't know what I meant, she wanted to scream. I just know that it's down to me to keep Mum safe and I can't do that if you make me start loving you all over again.

"I've been such a fool, Chloë," her father continued. "I did a terrible thing."

"Yes you did!" retorted Chloë, digging her fingernails into the palms of her hands. "And not for the first time either."

Her father pulled up at the traffic-lights.

"I promise you, darling, I will never, ever do such a thing again," he said. "You have to believe me – and you have to make Mum believe me."

"Why?" Chloë was sobbing now. "Why do we have to believe you? We've done that before and looked what happened!"

Her father put the car into gear and pulled away.

"I know," he sighed, holding a hand up to his forehead. "I know. But this time it's different. I've done a lot of thinking these last few weeks, made a lot of decisions."

Chloë glanced at him. His eyes were damp and despite herself she touched his arm.

"Like what?"

"Like I can't live without your mum!" To her horror, a

tear trickled down her father's cheek. "Like I'll do anything in the world to make things right! Without her, life has lost its meaning!"

Chloë bit her lip. He looked dreadful. And he really did seem sorry.

"I know now what went wrong," he continued. "I made work my god, got over-stressed, lost it totally."

"So what's to stop you doing that again?" demanded Chloë. "How do we know that the next time something goes wrong at work you won't lash out just like before?"

Her father winced. "Because I'm not going to carry on working all hours," he said. "I'm going to make Mum and you my priority."

He smiled anxiously at Chloë and his eyes crinkled at the edges just the way she remembered.

"Things really are going to change," he said. "You want us to be a happy family again, don't you?"

Yes, yes, yes, she cried silently. I want Mum to stop crying at nights, I want to be able to concentrate on my work again and I want to stop waking up with a jolt every time I hear a strange noise.

She nodded. "Yes, I do," she whispered.

But I'm not a kid.

I don't believe in happy endings any more.

The car turned the corner and Chloë suddenly realised they were almost at The Wharfside.

"And I know Mum misses me," he said, more confident now. "I can hear it in her voice when we speak on the phone."

Chloë nodded again. That bit was true. If Dad came back, and if it really did work, she wouldn't have to worry so much. And you were supposed to forgive people, and give them second chances – even third and fourth chances if you loved them.

"I don't expect Mum to believe me," her dad was saying, laying a hand on Chloë's knee, "but I can't prove it unless she gives me a chance."

He pulled the car on to the side of the road and switched off the engine.

"I want to come back, Chloë. I know it will work."

He opened the driver's door, walked round the front of the car and let Chloë out of the passenger seat.

"Talk to her, darling. For me. Please."

I can't, she thought wretchedly. I don't dare. I'm too scared.

"I'll try," she said and hated herself for being so weak.

She turned and began walking slowly towards the revolving doors of The Wharfside.

And stopped dead in her tracks. Turning the corner from the canal path, laden with shopping, was her mum.

No. Please. Don't look up. Not now. Not here.

"Chloë! Brilliant timing, you can help me with this load – oh! Edward!"

Her mum's gaze flew past Chloë to where her dad was still standing motionless at the side of the car.

For a moment no one moved. Then, from behind her, Chloë heard the familiar double beep as her father clicked his immobiliser and locked the car.

"Suzy!" he said and walked towards her. "Let me take that for you."

Chloë saw her mother hesitate and move back a couple of steps.

"It's OK," Chloë said hastily. "I'll do it – you go on, Mum."

Suzy looked at Chloë and then back at Edward. "Perhaps," she said tentatively, "you'd like to come in for a cup of tea?"

You're crazy! Chloë wanted to shriek. What are you doing?

But then she saw the look of hope on her mother's face and noticed the gentle way her father looked down at her.

After all, it was only a cup of tea. It couldn't do any harm to have a cup of tea together.

That's all it was.

Chapter 10

A WAY FORWARD?

SINEAD COULD hear the raised voices, from the bottom of the stairwell. She ran up the stairs two at a time and rammed her key into the lock.

"You had no right to do that, Kathleen, no right at all!" Her father's voice was unusually harsh.

"I had every right," she heard her mother retort. "Whose money is it, anyway?"

"Oh, we're back on that track, are we?" The kitchen door was flung open and Shaun stormed out and immediately tripped over a bucket and mop which were standing in the middle of the hallway.

"For heaven's sake!" he shouted. "Everywhere I go in this place, something's being cleaned. What's wrong with you?"

"Wrong with *me*? It's not me there's anything wrong with! If you would only . . ."

"MUM! DAD!" Sinead shouted, unzipping her jacket and throwing it on the hall table. "What's going on?"

"Nothing," they said in unison.

"Oh right!" snapped Sinead. "Get real."

"They're arguing about money." Erin appeared at the kitchen door, carrying a glass of blackcurrant, her face unusually pale. "Mum's hidden it."

"Hidden it?" Sinead frowned.

"I haven't hidden it, I've simply put it somewhere safe where your father can't keep frittering it away on silly schemes," she sniffed.

"And made me look an idiot, going to the bank to draw out money that wasn't there," interjected Shaun.

He sighed and put a tentative arm round Kathleen's shoulder. "Look, love, I only need a couple of thousand – I've got this great idea for decorated wheelbarrows and there's a job lot of old wooden ones going at auction. It's not much . . ."

"Not much? Would you have said it wasn't much when we were living at Burnthedge?"

"Things are different now, Kath," began her husband.

"Yes, you're right they're different!" To Sinead's horror, her mum burst into tears. "Different and horrid! I hate it! All of it!"

She wheeled round to go back into the kitchen and careered into Erin, who was leaning against the doorpost looking more and more anxious.

The glass was knocked out of her hand and a pool of purple juice spread across the carpet.

"Now look what you've done!" Kathleen grabbed a roll of kitchen towel and sank down on to her knees.

"It wasn't my fault!" Erin shouted. "Don't go blaming me!"

"Just go, get out of my way!" Kathleen waved her arm. "Just leave me alone! All of you!"

Sinead's father said nothing. He picked up his jacket and

walked through the hall and out of the front door.

Erin ran into her bedroom and slammed the door shut.

Sinead knelt down beside her mother and took the paper towel from her hand. "What is it, Mum?" she asked gently.

"This carpet . . . and your father and . . ."

"No, Mum," said Sinead, shaking her head. "Not that. What really is the matter?"

Kathleen looked at her daughter and Sinead held her gaze.

"I want things to be like they were," she whispered. "I hate being wealthy, Sinead. I hate it so much."

———

Poverty is the pits, thought Nick, hunching over his homework on the dining-room table and trying to blot out the sound of his grandmother singing her own particularly tuneless rendition of 'Danny Boy' in the kitchen. He could understand why people living in high-rise buildings suffered from stress; it was the lack of space that got to them. Like it's getting to me, he thought restlessly, shoving his books on one side and running his fingers through his hair. What the hell is the matter with me?

Even as he asked himself the question, he knew the answer. All his life, he had found his outlet in sport and now just when he needed it most he found himself at a school where rugby, rowing, running and hockey were unheard of, and there were only two periods of games in the whole week. He missed the matches on Saturday afternoons and the rivalry of the inter-house competitions each term. Lockbridge High didn't even have houses.

He gave up attempting his French translation and

switched on the television, zapping through the channels to avoid the countless advertisements for Christmas toys and CDs of carol music. Christmas was something he couldn't bear to think about. His gran kept dropping hints about what they might do, but neither he nor his mum showed any enthusiasm. How could they, now Dad wasn't here to share it?

He flicked on to another channel and paused as a soccer match came on screen.

"Sporty school kids across the county are getting into training for what has become one of the country's biggest school soccer competitions," announced the voice-over.

Nick punched the volume button and leaned forward to peer more closely at the screen.

"The All-Yorkshire Five-A-Side Festival started from humble beginnings ten years ago, and now attracts up to a hundred teams from a wide range of schools."

That was more like it – why hadn't Mr Carter told them about this?

"This year, following a major protest from footie-loving females, mixed teams will be allowed and the competition will take place at the end of January."

The camera panned in on the reporter.

"If your school hasn't entered yet, you had better hurry because the closing date is next Tuesday."

Tuesday? That was only a week away.

Mr Carter should be getting his act together.

He would tackle him in the morning. Because there was one thing of which Nick was absolutely certain.

This was too good an opportunity to miss. Lockbridge

had to enter a team, and he had to be on it.

And judging by the standard of soccer at Lockbridge High, he was pretty sure he could make it.

———

"I should have asked him to stay," said Chloë's mum for the fifth time in ten minutes. "I can't bear to think of him going back to that hotel all on his own."

"Mum . . ."

"He's lost weight, did you notice that? And his shirt collar wasn't ironed properly."

Chloë said nothing. It was true that her father had looked pale and drawn. What was more, he had seemed so much softer than usual.

"And you can tell he's changed," added Suzy eagerly. "We had a long talk while you were doing your homework and he really does mean things to be different."

"Oh yes?" muttered Chloë sarcastically, trying hard not to remember how good it felt when her father hugged her before leaving.

"And there's Christmas to think of and . . ." She paused as the telephone shrilled urgently.

"I'll get it," said Chloë, snatching up the receiver.

"Suzy darling! Nathan here!" Chloë frowned as a deep, gravelly voice boomed into her left ear. "I'm driving to your place with a bottle of bubbly and . . ."

"This isn't Suzy," snarled Chloë down the phone, glaring across the room at her mother. "This is her daughter."

"Oh, the enchanting Chloë!"

Oily creep, she thought.

"Pop your mum on to me then, there's a cherub!"

Chloë glowered at the receiver. "Mum," she said as loudly as she could, "there's a very rude man on the phone for you."

Her mother grabbed the phone and gave Chloë a withering look. "Suzy Sanderson speaking – oh, Nathan, it's you! Much better. So silly of me. Just tiredness. Dear of you to call, though."

Cut the TV-speak, thought Chloë.

"Dinner? Tonight? Well, I don't know really."

"The answer is no," hissed Chloë into her mother's left ear.

"Well, all right then, if you're sure you can put up with silly old me," simpered her mother.

"Oh puke!" muttered Chloë, sticking two fingers down her throat.

Her mother ignored her. "Twenty minutes? You're on! *Ciao*, Nathan!"

"Mum, who was that jerk? And why are you going out with him?"

Her mother frowned. "That was Nathan Reed, my producer, and he's not a jerk. He's a lovely man and he's been a real support to me since your dad – well, since everything happened."

"Well, don't be back late," ordered Chloë, stomping upstairs. "You've got to be up early in the morning."

She couldn't understand why her mother burst out laughing. It wasn't funny. She shouldn't be going anywhere with some strange man. It was obscene. She was a married woman.

At the moment.

But what if her mum got really keen on the Nathan guy and had an affair? What if she decided to divorce Dad and marry some awful man that Chloë didn't even know? It didn't bear thinking about.

Maybe she should have done what her dad asked and persuaded her mother to take him back.

It would be for the best, after all.

Anything would be better than Nathan Slimeball Reed.

———

"I suppose," sighed Sinead's mum as she sipped her fourth cup of tea, "that you think I'm being ridiculous?"

Sinead shook her head. "Of course I don't," she said. "I guess it's been a pretty big change for all of us."

Her mum looked at her in surprise.

"Yes, me too," admitted Sinead. "When I found out that Bianca and Abby were getting mega friendly just because they guessed I'd pay for everything we did, it hurt like hell. It still does sometimes."

"You never told me!" exclaimed her mother.

Sinead shrugged her shoulders. "I guess I felt a fool," she admitted. "It was my fault – I tried to buy their friendship."

Her mother frowned.

"Remember the jewellery I got in Majorca?" Sinead continued. "It was for them, not me."

Her mum nodded slowly. "With me, it's the opposite," she said. "I keep thinking that if I keep myself to myself, I'll cope. Everyone here is so grand . . ."

"They're not! Chloë's not grand . . ."

"I thought you two were deadly enemies," said her mother with a flicker of a smile.

"That was ages ago," said Sinead. "She's all right. So is her mum."

———

"I just feel so lonely," her mum sighed.

"So get a job," suggested Sinead. "You enjoyed being a dinner lady at Burnthedge Primary, didn't you?"

Her mum smiled. "Loved it," she said. "Oh, I know it wasn't brain surgery, but I loved being round all the children, and we all had a laugh and a natter . . ."

"So there you are!" Sinead said. "Get a job."

"Dad won't approve," Kathleen sighed. "He'll say that we don't need the money."

"What's that got to do with it?" demanded Sinead. "You wouldn't be doing it for the money. And all the money in the world is no use if you're unhappy, is it?"

Kathleen took her daughter's hand. "You know," she said, "you're right. How come I've got such a perceptive daughter?"

Sinead grinned. "I just say it how it is, I guess," she said.

"That," said her mum, "is what makes you so special."

Chapter 11

MAKING HEADWAY

"You look awful!" Jasmin gasped as Chloë pushed open the door of The Canal Café and yawned expansively.

"Oh thanks!" Chloë pulled a face. "Blame my mother – it was eleven-thirty before she got in, and then she wanted to tell me all about the menu in intricate detail. And talking of mothers, where's yours?"

"In the kitchen," said Jasmin. "Being neurotic because some guy sent back his breakfast. I take it you haven't changed your mind?"

"Why should I?"

Jasmin shrugged. "Rather you than me," she said.

Chloë pushed open the door of the kitchen and gestured to Jasmin to follow.

"Morning, Mrs Johnson!" she beamed.

"Hello, Chloë."

Chloë tried again. "You look lovely!"

"Oh yuk," muttered Jasmin.

"Thank you, dear," said Josie, loading a tray with hot croissants and unbending visibly. "Nice that you noticed –

more than can be said for my own family."

Chloë smiled again, so widely that she thought her lips would split. "Are you going somewhere special?"

"Oh, just a bit of shopping," said Jasmin's mum hastily. "Hadn't you better be going, you two? You don't want to miss the bus."

Chloë took a deep breath. "Actually, I wanted to ask you about the e-mail that arrived for me," she said sweetly. "Jasmin said it got destroyed – accidentally, of course – and I wondered if you could tell me what it said."

The smile vanished from Josephine's round face. "I think perhaps the least said about that, Chloë, the better," she remarked. "It wasn't exactly the sort of mail one expects a girl of sixteen to be receiving."

"Told you," muttered Jasmin. "Stand by for the sermon."

Josephine tipped some butter curls into a dish. "I don't know who it was from but . . ."

"Oh, I am quite sure it was from Jack," said Chloë calmly. "My boyfriend."

Josie swallowed. "Boyfriend?" she exclaimed, as if Chloë had just made her aware of the existence of a nest of vipers in her bedroom.

Chloë nodded. "He's nineteen and really sophisticated," she added proudly. "I met him in Greece."

"Nineteen? Greece?"

"That's what she said, Mum," interjected Jasmin.

Her mother frowned. "And your parents know about this?"

"Oh yes," said Chloë brightly. "They adore him – he's such a laugh."

Well, they quite liked him. In small doses. Well, Mum did. Some of the time.

"Indeed?" Mrs Johnson wasn't laughing.

"So if you could just tell me what the e-mail said . . ."

Josie wiped her hands on a tea towel. "I didn't read it word for word, it was far too explicit . . ."

Chloë's eyes widened hopefully.

". . . all I can recall is something about having a surprise for you, and missing you and something about hanging in there," she said rapidly and with an expression of pure distaste on her face. "And now I really think you should be going . . ."

"Thanks, Mrs Johnson," beamed Chloë. "That's really nice of you."

She turned to go.

"And Chloë?"

"Yes?"

"I don't approve of all this sort of thing, but I'm sorry I destroyed your message," said Josephine. "I just thought for one awful moment that Jasmin had got involved with some wayward boy."

"Mum!" Jasmin hissed at her mother.

"Oh no!" laughed Chloë. "You don't have to worry about Jasmin."

"I'm very pleased to hear it." Mrs Johnson smiled.

"She's only got eyes for Sanjay and he's hardly . . ." Chloë broke off, gasping as the toe of Jasmin's Kickers rammed into her shin.

"Must dash, Mum!" Jasmin hurtled out of the door without a backward glance.

"See you, Mrs Johnson!" called Chloë, running after her and letting the kitchen door slam behind her. "Wait for me, Jas!"

Jasmin dashed through the café, out the door and broke into a run along Millers Lane. By the time Chloë had caught up with her she was gasping for breath.

"Isn't it brilliant? Jack cares – he's got a surprise – that must be a late birthday pressie – when do you think it will come?"

Jasmin wheeled round and glared at her.

"I don't know and I don't care!" she stormed. "Did you have to go and talk about Sanjay?"

Chloë looked gobsmacked. "What's wrong with that? Everyone knows you two are joined at the hip."

Jasmin tossed her head in exasperation. "You don't understand," she said as they crossed the road to the bus stop. "My mum goes ballistic at the mention of his name."

"But why?" demanded Chloë. "You're nearly sixteen, for heaven's sake. And it's hardly as if Sanjay's the wild type, is it? What's to disapprove of?"

Jasmin bit her lip. "Sanjay's mixed race," she whispered. "His dad's white, his mum's Indian."

"So?"

"My parents don't approve of that kind of thing," she said. "They think black girls should go out with black boys."

"But that is so prejudiced!" exclaimed Chloë.

Jasmin shrugged. "Tell me about it," she said. "I know what's going to happen; she'll be checking up on me all the time, and I'll never get the chance to be alone with Sanjay."

To Chloë's horror, Jasmin was almost in tears.

She touched her arm. "I'm sorry," she said. "But don't worry – we can sort it."

"How?"

"I'll be your alibi," she said cheerfully. "Next time you and Sanjay want to get together, let me know and I'll sort it."

"Really?"

Jasmin looked doubtful.

"Trust me," confirmed Chloë. "I understand about these things. I know what it is to be in love."

———

"So I thought, sir, that we could enter some teams." Nick gave the head of PE one of his most winning smiles.

"Nice idea, Nick," sighed Mr Carter, pinning a Gym Club notice to the games board, "but hardly practical."

"Why, sir?"

"Because most of the schools who enter are way out of our league," he shrugged. "Lockbridge High doesn't have much of a sporting tradition."

"Then we must start one, sir," insisted Nick. "And this is a great way to do it."

Mr Carter frowned. "Nick, I don't have the time," he began. "There are no spaces in the timetable for practices . . ."

"We could do it after school."

"Oh great," rejoined Mr Carter, flicking a strand of greying hair from his left eye. "And I suppose I'm expected to organise all that as well as run the squash club, and help Mrs Hood coach the GCSE dance team and drag Year Seven back and forth to the local pool and . . ."

"I could do it, sir," Nick heard himself say. "I ran for my old school, and was vice captain of rugby."

"Very commendable, I'm sure," sighed Mr Carter. "But you have your GCSE mock exams to think of . . ."

"But, sir, the competition will be over by then. And you wouldn't have to get involved. I know I could do it, sir."

"And what could you do, Nicholas?"

Nick turned to see Mr Lamport, the headmaster, eyeing him quizzically.

Nick launched into his proposal all over again.

"And we could enter mixed teams, sir," he finished, knowing how very hot Mr Lamport was on equality for all.

The headmaster tapped his nose and looked thoughtful. "You know," he said. "I think that might be a very good idea."

"I don't think . . ." began Mr Carter, bristling with annoyance.

"I do," affirmed Mr Lamport. "But it will all be down to you, Nicholas."

"Brilliant! Thank you, sir."

Nick sped off down the hall.

"Headmaster, I really do feel that this is not a good idea," began Mr Carter.

"You're wrong, Geoffrey," said the head. "Anything that makes Nicholas Bowen look happy for the first time since he joined us, has to be a very good idea indeed."

Chapter 12

THE THINGS WE DO FOR LOVE

"How can you sound so cheerful after double Science?" asked Sinead, as Nick jumped down the stairs to the canteen two at a time, humming the latest Chaotic hit. "It's obscene!"

Nick grinned. "Mr Lamport says we can enter teams in the Yorkshire Schools Five-A-Side competition," he said. "And he's put me in charge."

"Great," said Sinead, wondering why Nick sounded as excited as if he had just won the Lottery.

"I knew it would be your sort of thing," he beamed. "Which is why I want you at the trials."

"Trials?"

"For the team, silly," said Nick. "We're entering two mixed teams – that way we stand more chance of getting somewhere. What do you say?"

"I can't play football."

"Nor can any of the girls," he reasoned. "You run, though, don't you?"

Only when I'm chasing you, Sinead thought, and then it takes me a week to recover.

"And you're fit?"

Not half as fit as you are, she sighed to herself, gazing at his broad shoulders.

She inclined her head in a non-committal fashion.

"Of course, it would mean coming to all the practices," he said.

"And you'd be in charge?"

Nick nodded. "I guess you don't really have time," he began.

"Oh I do," she said eagerly. "All the time in the world. When's the trial?"

———

"You are *what*?" Chloë almost choked on her three bean casserole. "But you hate sport!"

"Keep your voice down!" retorted Sinead, glancing anxiously across the canteen to where Nick was regaling a group of Year Tens. "Actually, I've been thinking for ages that I ought to get more exercise!"

Chloë giggled. "I bet the sort of exercise you really want doesn't take place on a muddy field in the middle of winter," she grinned. "You're only doing it because of Nick."

Sinead pulled a face and eyed Chloë closely. "So are you going to try for the team too?" she asked casually.

"No way!" exploded Chloë. "I can't think of anything worse."

"Oh good," said Sinead.

"Pardon?"

"Nothing."

Sanjay and Jasmin sat in the corner of the library pretending to be engrossed in an encyclopaedia.

"Can't we see one another tonight?" Sanjay pleaded. "I mean, if I can't come round to your place, why don't we go out somewhere?"

Jasmin hesitated.

"You wouldn't have to be alone in the dark," said Sanjay. "I'd wait for you round the corner and bring you home again."

He was so thoughtful, she thought. And so gorgeous.

And Chloë was right – she was almost sixteen. No way could she let her mother's stupid ideas blight her entire life.

"What about homework?"

"Just an hour – we could have a coffee and then you could go back," suggested Sanjay. "Anything just to be together."

He was so romantic.

"OK," she said, her brain working overtime. "But it will have to be straight after school."

"Anything," agreed Sanjay.

"You're on," smiled Jasmin.

———

"Chloë, wait!" Jasmin panted across the school yard and grabbed her friend's arm. "You know you said you'd be my alibi?"

Chloë nodded. "Of course," she said. "Just tell me when."

"Now."

"So what do you want me to do?"

Jasmin frowned. "You're the one with the good ideas," she said. "I want to spend some time with Sanjay and I need you to pretend to my mum that I'm somewhere else."

Chloë bit her lip. "Shopping?"

Jasmin shook her head. "She'll moan about me being extravagant."

"Detention?"

"Get real! That's a hangable offence in our house!"

Chloë snapped her fingers. "Got it!" she said.

"Well?" demanded Jasmin.

"I'll tell her you want to be in the five-a-side team and you've stayed behind to find out more about it," she said.

"I don't want to be in it," Jasmin protested.

"That's neither here nor there, is it?" reasoned Chloë. "Your mum will be well pleased, especially if I drop in the fact about Sanjay being totally useless at sport. And you can use the practices as cover for seeing Sanjay."

Jasmin frowned. "But what will happen when the competition comes and I'm not playing?"

"Fake an injury," said Chloë with a grin.

Jasmin beamed. "That's mega!" she said. "Well done, you!"

Chloë smiled and shrugged. "One aims to please."

———

"You are wicked!" laughed Sinead as she and Chloë left The Canal Café. " 'Oh yes, Mrs Johnson, Jasmin's got really keen on football lately; Sanjay, Mrs Johnson? Oh no, he's not remotely interested in things like that. I guess Jasmin's going to be really busy, Mrs Johnson, now she's involved in the competition.' "

"It worked," agreed Chloë. "She even apologised to me for coming on strong about the e-mail from Jack."

"What e-mail?" asked Sinead, thinking that it might be politic not to let on that Jasmin had mentioned it.

Chloë told her.

"So you think it might still be on with you and Jack, then?" asked Sinead as calmly as she could.

"Oh yes," enthused Chloë. "I just wish he wasn't hundreds of miles away."

You, thought Sinead with a sigh, are not the only one.

Chapter 13

ENCOUNTER IN THE CORN EXCHANGE

FOR THE next few days, things went rather more smoothly for most of the friends. Jasmin's mother appeared delirious with joy at the thought of her daughter engaging in what she called a healthy outdoor activity, and since Jasmin had the foresight to smear her games kit with an appropriate amount of mud and to start hobbling slightly, complaining of stiffness due to the unaccustomed amount of exercise, she was able to keep up the pretence even though Nick hadn't held his first practice yet.

As for Sanjay, by Friday morning, he was beginning to think that he might be turning into a normal sort of guy. Whenever he held Jasmin's hand, he felt a great surge of something remarkably like what was described in Chapter Three of *So You Think You're in Love?* and when, on Thursday, he dared to kiss her on the lips for the first time, she didn't pull away, but linked her hands behind his neck and hung on for dear life. Which was really rather enjoyable.

Nick felt better than he had for weeks. At last it seemed as if he was in charge of at least a small part of his life. He had posted lists all round the school, asking potential players to sign up, and had fixed the date for the team trials. Now all he needed to do was to work out a fitness programme that everyone would have to follow. There was going to be nothing half-hearted about this; everyone would have to go for runs just like he did, and work out till they were in peak condition. Like his old school motto said: he who strives wins.

Sinead alternated between the heights of euphoria every time Nick talked to her and the slough of despond when she thought about the forthcoming trials. She loathed sport; in fact, she was the school expert on excuses for dodging everything from swimming to squash. She wished she'd tried harder; if she didn't get on the team, didn't get the chance to be with Nick for all the practices, she would die.

Chloë's week was rather more of a rollercoaster ride. For one thing, there was no sign of any sort of surprise from Jack; nothing in the post and no phonecalls. She was getting very worried; for all she knew, he had asked her to call him in Greece, or needed her to do something for him, and because of Jasmin's mother she would never know. What was worse was that because Josephine had been so stuffy about the e-mail, there was no chance that she and Jasmin could sneak into the office and send Jack another one. They had thought about doing it if Josephine went out – but she never did. She seemed glued to the café and because of that, Chloë's whole destiny hung in the balance.

And as if that wasn't enough anxiety for one week, her mum had seen The Slimeball again on Wednesday, only this time he had come to the flat for supper and gushed all over Chloë and tried to pretend he was a world authority on everything from the pop scene to London Fashion Week. He kept patting Suzy's hand and calling her his little star, which made Chloë want to throw up all over his hideous grey patent leather shoes. She had tried to explain to her mother that she was a married woman with responsibilities, but Suzy had just laughed and told Chloë it was just a bit of harmless fun and that Nathan was a married man who behaved like that with all the female presenters. As if that made it better. It was amazing what dual standards parents could have when it came to morality.

On Thursday, just as she was beginning to think that she had been seriously wrong in discouraging her mother from seeing more of her dad, Edward turned up on the doorstep, clutching a huge bouquet of flowers and a bottle of champagne. She had been almost glad when he ended up staying for supper, especially as he cooked one of his wicked Thai curries. Not, of course, that she could risk leaving the two of them alone; which meant another load of homework was late and Mrs Reilly was turning puce every time she met Chloë in the corridor. But her mum had gone even more soft and gooey with him than with the dreaded Nathan, and if anyone was going to put a smile back on her mother's face, Chloë decided that it had to be Dad. Life with Slimeball was definitely not on.

"I've got a problem," Sinead told Chloë at lunch on Friday.

"Only one?" muttered Chloë who had just had a rather verbal encounter with Mr Tompkins over the matter of the non-appearance of her Maths homework and received a B- for the English essay. "Lucky you!"

"You have to come into town with me after school," Sinead continued. "I need to buy shorts."

"Shorts? In November?" Chloë stared at her incredulously.

"For the football trials," Sinead explained. "My games shorts make my bottom look fat."

"Wear a track suit over the top," suggested Chloë.

"Get real! They are the most unsexy garments on earth."

Chloë raised an eyebrow. "Oh, so that's it, is it?" she grinned. "Never mind the footwork, watch the sexy hip swing!"

Sinead blushed a livid shade of beetroot. "Only teasing," said Chloë kindly. "Of course I'll come."

"Come where?" said Nick, pulling back a chair and dumping a plate of chicken pie on the table.

Chloë caught Sinead's warning glance. "Wherever we all decide to go tomorrow night," she improvised hastily.

"Any ideas?" Nick looked eagerly at Chloë.

"Fat Harry's?"

"Brilliant!" agreed Nick. "Shall I pick you up?"

"She'll come with me," interjected Sinead instantly. "We'll meet you there. OK?"

"OK," sighed Nick.

———

"I can't wait for tomorrow night," Sinead said as they walked down Vicar Lane.

"I might not bother coming," shrugged Chloë. "It's OK for you, having Nick to drool over, but I'll be on my own. Again."

"Missing Jack?" asked Sinead. The fact that Chloë had

assumed she and Nick would be doing some drooling made her feel unusually charitable.

Chloë nodded. "And it's worse knowing that he tried to get in touch and . . . oh my God! Sinead! Look! Oh my God!"

She grabbed Sinead's arm and stared, wild-eyed, across the street.

"What is it? What's the matter?"

Chloë clamped her hands to her face. "It's him! It's him!"

"Who's him?"

"Over there – in the leather jacket. It's Jack! I don't believe it!"

She began jumping up and down as a bus pulled up at the stop opposite and blocked her view.

"Oh no, I can't see him!" she cried. "Come on – quickly!"

She grabbed Sinead's arm, dashed off the kerb and leaped back as a taxi driver honked and waved his fist at her.

"Hang on!" protested Sinead. "Are you sure it's him? I mean, it can happen – you think about someone so much that you start imagining you see them."

"I didn't imagine it," insisted Chloë, dragging Sinead through the traffic as the bus pulled away. She cast her eyes up and down the street. "He's gone!"

Sinead sighed. "Chloë, he's in Greece, for heaven's sake . . ."

"No, the season will be over now!" Chloë scanned the street once more.

"So he's come home," reasoned Sinead. "And where did you say he lived?"

"Devon," said Chloë.

"Precisely," said Sinead. "So is it really likely . . . ?"

Sinead was prevented from ending her sentence by an ear-splitting shriek in her left ear.

"Look! Over there! I told you so! It is him – it's really, really him!"

"Really? Wow!"

It suddenly occurred to Sinead that if it *was* Jack, and he and Chloë got together, Nick would need a lot of love and understanding when he heard the news. She thought she might be rather good at that.

"He's going into the Corn Exchange," gabbled Chloë, grabbing Sinead's arm. "Come on!"

She set off at a run, dodging the late afternoon shoppers. By the time they had run up the steps and into the crowded Corn Exchange, Sinead was gasping for breath. So much for being fit for football, she thought.

"There are so many people," complained Chloë, craning her head to peer over the crowds at all the stalls and little boutiques which filled the ground floor.

"Is that him?" asked Sinead, gesturing to a tall, broad-shouldered guy who was rifling through a rack of CDs on a brightly painted wheelbarrow.

Chloë let out another high-pitched squeal and then clamped her hand over her mouth. "Yes!" she squeaked. "Isn't he divine?"

"Well, go on, then," urged Sinead, giving her a gentle shove. "Go and say hi!"

Chloë shook her head and dashed to hide behind a pillar. "I can't," she said. "He mustn't see me!"

Sinead looked gobsmacked. "Chloë," she said pointedly. "For the last two months, you have been wittering on, day after day, about wanting to see Jack. Now he's right in front of you and you behave like a frightened rabbit."

Chloë sighed impatiently. "I'm in school uniform," she explained. "I look a real saddo."

Sinead sighed and raised her eyebrows. "OK," she said. "This way."

"What . . . ?"

"Don't argue," ordered Sinead. "Just come."

———

"You look fantastic!" Sinead stood back to survey the new Chloë. She was wearing an ankle length shaggy fun fur coat, a striped beanie hat and yellow waffle scarf. Not one inch of her school uniform showed.

"Can my friend just have a bit of saunter round?" Sinead boldly asked the boutique assistant. "You know – to get the feel of the clothes?"

The assistant looked doubtful.

"Here!" Sinead grabbed Chloë's wrist and took off her Gucci watch. "Keep this as a guarantee that we'll be back. Her mother's Suzy Sanderson, you know."

Before the assistant could open her mouth, Sinead had dragged Chloë away.

"That's a fake Gucci," Chloë hissed, trying desperately not to fall over the hem of her coat. "My dad brought it back from Bangkok."

"She won't know," shrugged Sinead. "Look, he's still there – go on, strut your stuff!"

Chloë gulped. "Come with me," she pleaded.

Sinead grinned and marched towards Jack. "Go on," she hissed at Chloë.

Chloë took a deep breath and rammed her beanie hat further down on her head. "What shall I say?" she mouthed.

"Oh, for heaven's sake," muttered Sinead. "Just do it."

Chloë took a deep breath and tapped Jack on the back. "Hi, Jack!" she said brightly.

Jack turned, an expression of surprise on his face. "I'm sorry?"

Chloë grinned. "It's me!"

"Oh my goodness! It's you!" He scanned her face. "It's not? It can't be?" he exclaimed after a minute. "It's – tell me it is you."

"It is me," Chloë laughed. "Chloë!"

"Chloë!" he repeated, clapping his hands to his mouth. "This is unbelievable!"

"What are you doing here?" Chloë asked, unable to take her eyes off his face.

"I was just thinking about you, actually!" Jack said suddenly, opening his arms and giving her a hug.

Chloë felt her face burn as her heart began to race.

"You were?"

Jack threw back his head and laughed, revealing two rows of perfectly even white teeth. "Not that there's anything strange about that," he said. "I think about you a great deal."

Chloë's knees seemed unwilling to carry on with the job of supporting her body. "When you didn't write, I thought . . ." Chloë hesitated. All the magazines said you shouldn't make them think you cared.

"Didn't write?" Jack's eyes opened wide in astonishment. "You didn't get my letters?"

Chloë shook her head.

"Honestly," Jack retorted, "the Greek mail is diabolical. I wrote to you three times. I was so disappointed that you hadn't been in touch . . ."

"But I wrote . . ."

"I never got a letter," sighed Jack.

"What about the phone message? This girl – she said . . ."

"Phone? Oh, well, those girls in reception were useless," he said quickly.

Chloë nodded with relief. "I got your message anyway – well, sort of," she said.

"Message?" Jack's sun-tanned face puckered into a frown.

"The e-mail," she added.

"The e-mail? You got the e-mail?"

Chloë nodded and then sighed. "Well, to be honest, it got binned before I read it. Sorry."

"Oh, don't be sorry," Jack said quickly. "Although it was pretty poetic stuff, even if I say so myself."

He picked up a CD and scrutinised it closely.

"Ask him about the surprise!" hissed Sinead, deserting the jewellery stall where she had been loitering and appearing at Chloë's elbow.

"Shut up!" Chloë muttered back.

"Well, hello there!" Jack turned at the sound of Sinead's voice and gave her a sparkling smile. "And you are . . . ?"

"Sinead – Chloë's best mate," said Sinead firmly. "You said you had a surprise for her."

"Sinead!" Chloë gasped.

"I did? I mean, I do, I do – well, I did," said Jack hastily. "Only it's spoiled now."

Chloë frowned. "How come?"

"The surprise," he said slowly, taking Chloë's hand and giving it a squeeze, "was me. I was going to turn up on your birthday. At your house."

"Flat," said Sinead. "And her birthday was last month."

"SINEAD!" Chloë glared at her. "That's really sweet, Jack," she continued, fluttering her eyelashes ever so subtly and running her tongue along her bottom lip. "Thank you."

Jack looked devastated. "I've missed it? Your birthday?"

Chloë nodded.

"Oh, Chloë, I'm so sorry," he said. "I was so sure it was – er, November the twenty-eighth."

"October the sixteenth," said Chloë.

"Sugar," said Jack. "Not that I would have been here anyway – I only got back on Monday."

"So has the job in Greece finished?" asked Chloë, relieved to discover that she had regained the power of coherent speech. Jack nodded.

"They begged me to stay for the winter season," he said. "Told me I was their most popular instructor. But, to be honest, I can do better for myself than teaching dippy teenagers to sail. Not that you, of course, came into that category. You were – are – something else."

He flashed her another winning smile.

Chloë's stomach lurched uncontrollably.

"So what are you doing in Leeds?" asked Chloë.

"Well, actually . . ." Jack began.

"Excuse me." A woman with auburn hair tapped her on

the shoulder. "Are you going to buy those clothes or not?"

"Just coming," said Chloë hastily, holding the coat closed and not moving an inch.

"Before you go," began Jack earnestly, "when can I see you again?"

Chloë paused and tried to look indifferent. "I'll be at Fat Harry's tomorrow evening," she said, failing hopelessly.

"We both will," interjected Sinead.

"Fat Harry's?" Jack looked puzzled.

"It's a club, down at Granary Wharf," Chloë explained.

"Oh right," Jack nodded. "Well, perhaps . . ."

"The clothes, if you don't mind, miss!" The assistant was back and this time she had given up trying to look friendly.

"Right," said Chloë reluctantly. "I'd better go, Jack."

"Me too," he said, glancing at his watch. "But not before I have a kiss."

He cupped her chin in his hands and planted a light kiss on her lips. "I simply can't believe it's you."

Chloë thought she might very well die from sheer happiness.

"Will I see you tomorrow?" she breathed.

She knew it was uncool to ask but she had to know.

"Just you try and stop me," he said. "I can't wait."

———

"I'm so happy!" breathed Chloë, shrugging her arms out of the coat and handing it back to the weary-looking assistant. "Isn't he divine? Don't you think he's good-looking? Do you think he still likes me?"

"Yes, yes and undoubtedly yes," grinned Sinead. "Now please can we go and look for shorts?"

Chloë nodded happily and linked her arm through Sinead's. They crossed the street and headed for Shelf Space. They were about to go into the store when a slim girl with waist-length blonde hair and a to-die-for pair of knee-high boots brushed past them, waving frantically.

"Jackie! Hey, Jackie, over here!"

As one, Chloë and Sinead turned to follow her gaze.

She was waving directly at a tall guy waiting on the street corner.

It was Jack.

"Who's that?" Chloë gasped, clutching at Sinead's arm.

Jack looked up and grinned as the girl tottered over to him and slipped her arm through his.

And then she ruffled his dark curly hair with her hand and gave him a squeeze.

"Who the hell does she think she is?" exploded Chloë. "I'll kill her."

Jack stepped into the road and flagged down a taxi. And then, far too tenderly for Chloë's liking, he helped the girl into the back seat and climbed in beside her.

Chloë gulped and looked at Sinead.

"What you have to remember," Sinead said firmly, as much to reassure herself as to calm her friend, "is that he said he couldn't wait to see you tomorrow. That girl's probably just an old family friend. He was probably just being polite."

"You really think so?" pleaded Chloë.

"I'm sure of it," said Sinead.

And wished she was.

Just at the time when Sinead was trying on a pair of particularly skimpy denim shorts, Sanjay was on the phone to Jasmin.

"You will come to Fat Harry's tomorrow, won't you?" he pleaded. "I mean, your mum won't stop you this time?"

"No way," affirmed Jasmin. "I've worked out a plan. It's foolproof. But you have to meet me there because I'll be getting my dad to drop me off."

"OK," agreed Sanjay. "Eight o'clock?"

"I can't wait," said Jasmin.

Chapter 14

ON THE UP?

"MUM! You'll never guess what!"

Chloë slammed the front door and tore into the sitting-room.

"We were out shopping and . . . what on earth?"

The sitting-room floor was strewn with designer carrier bags and boxes brimming over with tissue paper.

"I've had a little spending spree," beamed Suzy, lifting the lid off one of the boxes. "Ta-rah!"

She held up an emerald green evening dress, scattered with sequins.

"Wow! That's lovely!" breathed Chloë.

"And look, there's this . . ." She produced an embroidered silk and velvet scarf.

". . . and this . . ." Out came a black, feather-trimmed evening bag.

"And aren't these to die for?" She slipped a pair of strappy gold sandals on to her feet.

"Sensational!" agreed Chloë. "Now listen, Mum, you'll never guess who . . ."

"I thought I'd wear them to the awards ceremony," chattered her mother. "I want to look my best."

She fiddled with a shoe strap and took a deep breath. "Dad says he'll come with me," she said in a rush. "So that's lovely, isn't it?"

"Dad!" Chloë gasped. "But . . ."

She paused.

If her father was there, at least Nathan Reed wouldn't get a look-in. Dad was very possessive of her mother. Mum did look ecstatic about the idea.

"Nothing permanent," said her mum hastily. "Just for the evening."

"But what if he . . . ?" She couldn't bring herself to say it.

"Darling, the media will be out in force, and it would look strange if Dad wasn't there, especially since he is so well-known in TV circles."

"I guess," agreed Chloë.

"I would have taken you, darling, but really you'd be frightfully bored."

"That's OK," said Chloë. "It's not my scene. And it's lovely that Dad's coming."

She was rewarded with one of her mother's glittering smiles.

It would be fine, she told herself. After all, nothing could happen in a public place. And besides, Dad did seem to have changed.

"Now, darling," said her mother, "what was it you were going to say?"

"I saw Jack today," she said.

"Jack?"

"From Greece," said Chloë impatiently.

"Oh, that Jack." Her mother sounded less than ecstatic.

Chloë tossed her head and ignored her. "That's who I'm going out with tomorrow – to Fat Harry's," she continued.

While her mother exclaimed, and started plying her with questions, Chloë tried very hard to reassure herself that, from now on, with Jack back and Dad and Mum doing things together again, everything really was going to be hunky-dory.

———

"Dad," said Sinead as they laid the table for supper. "Why don't you take Mum out tomorrow night?"

"Why? Want some friends over, do you?" grinned her father.

"No," asserted Sinead. "It's just that – well, Mum's not very happy at the moment."

"Tell me about it," sighed her father. "I don't understand it. She's got this lovely home, all these wonderful things . . ."

"But don't you see, Dad – everything's turned upside-down," explained Sinead. "She used to go out to work . . ."

"You're not trying to tell me she'd like to be a dinner lady again!"

"At least then she had mates to chat to and things to keep her busy," said Sinead. "Now she feels out of place and lonely – me and Erin are at school, you're at the workshop and she's got nothing."

Her father frowned. "But we don't need the money," he reasoned. "I don't approve of people taking jobs away from those who really need to earn."

"You do," Sinead pointed out.

"My furniture decorating is just a hobby that will hopefully pay its way," he countered. "Besides, I've always worked and I'd be like a fish out of water if I didn't have something to get my teeth into."

"Exactly!" said Sinead. "And Mum's no different, and that's why she cleans all the time. I've read about it."

"Quite the little psychologist, aren't you?" smiled her father, not unkindly. "I'll tell you what – I'll talk to Mum about it and find out just what she wants to do. Maybe I'll cook her dinner for a change, or take her out somewhere. But you'll have to baby-sit Erin."

"No way!" exploded Sinead. "I'll be out."

"So take Erin with you," said her father. "Mum won't want her to be left on her own."

"You have to be joking," protested Sinead. "We're going to Fat Harry's – she's too young."

"I heard that!" Erin stuck her head round the door. "And actually, so are you! You're supposed to be sixteen and you're only fifteen and three-quarters."

"And you," hissed Sinead, "won't reach thirteen if you don't shut up!"

———

"Nick was singing while I got changed for work," Jenny Bowen observed to Josephine as they served drinks together behind the bar.

"You make it sound like the eighth wonder of the world," laughed Josie.

"Believe me, it is!" replied Jenny. "Apparently, he's organising some mixed football competition . . ."

"Oh yes, Jasmin's over the moon about that, too,"

nodded Josie, squirting some lemonade into a customer's shandy. "Amazes me – she's never shown much interest in sport before."

"And he's off to a club tomorrow night," Jenny went on. "It really seems as if he's getting a life at last."

"Don't you mind?"

"What? That he's getting a life? Far from it!"

"No – him to going to clubs, I mean," said Josie.

Jenny shrugged and unscrewed a bottle of black olives. "I trust him," she said. "And besides, he's sixteen. I can't hang on to him for ever."

"I guess you're right," said Josephine in tones that suggested she was positively certain Jenny was wrong. "I just wish sometimes that I could turn the clock back, have things back the way they used to be."

"Me too," murmured Jenny softly, but Josie appeared not to have heard her.

"I can't take much more of this, you know," Josie went on, filling some glass dishes with taco chips. "I feel like my whole life has been put on hold since Harry's accident. When he was out driving taxis, I was able to do my own thing and now . . ."

"At least Harry's alive!" The words were out before Jenny could stop them. "At least this place is turning out to be a little gold mine. I can't see what's so hard about it all!"

Josie gasped.

"I envy you, do you know that?" Jenny went on, unable to stop now that the floodgates had opened. "Living here, building up the business, meeting new people every day. I'd give anything to be in your shoes!"

Josie touched her arm. "Jenny, I'm sorry, I just didn't think," she began.

"It's OK!" Jenny shrugged her off and nodded to a customer who was beckoning her to take an order. "Bad day – sorry."

She grabbed her notepad and headed for the corner table.

Josie looked after her thoughtfully.

"I wonder," she muttered, under her breath. "I just wonder."

Chapter 15

CONFLICTING
PASSIONS

"HI, FAITH? It's me, Jasmin. Look, I wondered if you fancied a night out together? It's been ages."

Jasmin clutched the telephone and crossed her fingers.

"Oh yes, of course Shelley can come too. Make it the three of us, like we used to. You would? Brilliant!"

Thank you, God.

"I thought Fat Harry's." She crossed the fingers of her other hand. "It's a really cool place. You will? Great!"

Careful now, she told herself.

"Actually, why don't we make a real evening of it?" she gabbled. "You and Shelley come here for supper first – my mum's always saying she doesn't see enough of you and it won't cost you. Six-thirty? See you then!"

There were times, she told herself happily as she replaced the handset on its stand, when she was really rather brilliant.

———

"Mum, I've asked Faith and Shelley over for supper – is that OK?" Jasmin smiled endearingly.

"That's lovely, dear," enthused her mother. "Such delightful girls."

"And then we're going out," ventured Jasmin.

Her mother opened her mouth but Jasmin was too quick for her. "You were right, Mum – I haven't seen enough of them lately, and they're such fun," she said. "We thought we'd pop into Fat Harry's for a bit."

"Fat Harry's?"

"It's an under-eighteen night," replied Jasmin, putting the emphasis on the under-eighteen bit. "Faith's mum says they're a brilliant idea – Tony's been there loads of times."

"Well," said Josie, "if Mrs Carmichael approves, that's good enough for me. Such an elegant lady."

Jasmin wondered what dress sense had to do with it, but merely smiled in a well-behaved sort of way.

"You have a good time, darling," continued her mother magnanimously. "Will any of your other friends be there?"

Jasmin opened her eyes as wide as she could. "I honestly don't know, Mum," she said, as if such a thought hadn't crossed her mind. "But me and Faith and Shelley just want a good gossipy girls' night out. Nothing more."

She knew lying was a sin, but it was a lot less risky than telling her mother the truth.

And besides, what she didn't know wouldn't hurt her.

Not just this once.

———

"Are you sure I look OK?" Chloë asked Sinead for the fifth time.

"You look great," Sinead assured her.

"Not too tarty?"

"No."

"Or too twee?"

"No."

"But just a bit sexy, you think? I mean, as sexy as that girl he met and . . ."

"Chloë!" Sinead exploded. "You look amazing, fantastic, alluring . . . satisfied? Only it might all have been for nothing."

Chloë gasped. "What do you mean?"

"If you don't get a move on, Jack'll be fed up with waiting."

Chloë grabbed her clutch bag and sped down the stairs. "Bye, Mum!" she said, planting a kiss on the top of her mother's head. "We're off!"

Suzy smiled. "Are you sure your father is happy to fetch you both, Sinead dear? I don't like to think of you wandering the streets late at night."

Sinead nodded.

"And, Chloë dear, be careful, won't you? Don't put your drink down anywhere, and stick with people you know, and don't let Jack come on too strong – you don't really know him and . . ."

"MUM!"

"Sorry, dear."

———

Nick stood under the shower and let the hot water wash over him. It had been a good day; he had run ten kilometres, including some pretty challenging terrain, and he felt great. Forty-six people had signed up for the football trials on Monday – mainly boys, it was true, but he was sure he could knock the few keen girls into shape.

And in less than an hour he would be with Chloë.

All the time he had been running, he'd been practising what he would say. Of course, he realised now where he had been going wrong – he hadn't come on strong enough. Well, tonight he would tell her. The bit about her eyes and how the day seemed brighter when he was with her.

He liked that bit.

He'd heard it on 'Love Lines' on Radio One and been very impressed.

He stepped from the shower and began towelling himself briskly.

He knew that once he and Chloë were an item, he'd feel completely normal again. Look at Sanjay; he was a new man since Jasmin came on the scene.

"Nothing like the love of a good woman, son!" His father's voice echoed in his memory. "You'll find that out soon enough."

You're right, Dad, he said silently in his head.

And tonight's the night.

————

"He's not here!" Chloë looked wildly round the dimly-lit club. "It's half past eight and he's not here!"

Sinead patted her arm comfortingly. "He'll come," she assured her. "After all, you never agreed a time."

"Do you think I should have?" gasped Chloë. "What if he doesn't come? What if he's gone out with that girl? What if . . . oh!"

She wheeled round as a hand tapped her shoulder. It was Nick.

"Oh," she said flatly. "Hi."

"I've bought you a drink." Nick flashed her a smile. "Sparkling apple juice – I know you like that."

"Thanks," she said, taking a long draught.

"Hi, Nick!" For some reason Sinead's voice had dropped two octaves and taken on a husky tone. "How's things?"

"Fine," he said. "Chloë, come and dance."

He grabbed her arm.

"No, thanks." Chloë's eyes were still darting round the club.

"Oh come on," urged Nick.

"Later maybe," murmured Chloë, edging towards the door. "Why don't you dance with Sinead?"

"Oh. Right." Nick didn't move.

"You'll be quite safe," sighed Sinead, as Chloë moved away. "My feet are very well trained."

Nick grinned. "I love your sense of humour," he said. "Come on, then, I suppose we might as well give it a go. They say dancing is a great way to get fit."

Getting fit, thought Sinead, is currently the last thing on my mind. And I am clearly the last thing on yours.

———

"You know Sanjay, don't you?" Jasmin turned to Faith and Shelley. "And this is Chloë."

"Hi," said Chloë, glancing at them before turning her attention to the door of the club.

"Stuck-up cow," muttered Shelley in Faith's ear.

"We'll just get some drinks," Jasmin said. "Grab some seats, Shelley."

She marched over to the bar, followed by Sanjay.

"What did you have to bring them for?" he demanded.

"I want you to myself."

"They're my alibi, silly," explained Jasmin. "As long as Mum thinks I'm with them, she'll be cool about me coming out."

"Does that mean that whenever we go anywhere, they have to tag along too?" Sanjay sounded dejected.

Jasmin shook her head. "It's only for tonight," she assured him, grabbing the drinks and heading back towards the table. "After that, she'll just assume. Now are you going to ask me to dance or not?"

———

"So will you dance now?" Nick asked Chloë.

"OK," she sighed.

Jack wasn't going to come. It was obvious.

It was only a matter of time before she died of a broken heart.

She followed Nick on to the dance floor and tried to gyrate with a modicum of enthusiasm.

"You look lovely," he told her, taking her hands and pulling her closer to him.

"Thanks," she said, pulling back slightly. "So are you all clued up for this football thing?"

"Mmm," he nodded.

"You're really keen on sport, aren't you?" she asked.

"Not nearly as keen as I am on – Chloë, where are you going?"

"Sorry – back in a minute!"

Nick stood in the centre of the floor, with couples twirling and raving all round him.

He watched, rooted to the spot, as Chloë rushed up to a

tall guy with curly dark hair who spun round and wrapped her in a hug.

And then kissed her.

Full on the lips.

For what seemed an eternity.

———

Nick stared at the floor and slouched back to his seat.

He didn't want to look at what Chloë was doing, but his eyes appeared to have taken on a life of their own and kept swivelling back to where she and this hateful guy were standing arm-in-arm, laughing happily.

Before he knew it, his fist had slammed on to the table, making the lemonade in his glass splash over the marble top.

What a dork! To think that Chloë was available, that he had any kind of chance with her.

He should have guessed.

That guy looked twenty if he was a day and he didn't have a zit in sight.

Nick didn't know who he was, or where he came from.

All he knew was that right now, he would have given anything to be standing where he was.

———

"Of course I came, sweetheart!"

Jack smiled down at Chloë as they danced, arms wrapped tightly round one another in the centre of the room.

"And you've really missed me?"

"Like crazy," he assured her, cupping her chin in his hands and kissing her again.

Chloë's whole body tingled as she ran her fingers through his hair.

"Yesterday, after we left," she ventured, "I saw you with this girl."

"Natalie," he said, nodding.

"Who's Natalie?" asked Chloë through gritted teeth.

"Why? Not jealous, surely?" He grinned down at her.

"No." To Chloë's annoyance, her denial came out as a high-pitched squeak.

"Good," said Jack. "Because I've known her for ages, and we're really close."

"Oh!"

This time the squeak was even more strangled.

Jack laughed. "Don't worry, darling," he teased. "Nat's my sister."

"Your *sister?*" Chloë exclaimed, her heart soaring. "That's wonderful! I mean, that's nice."

Jack nodded. "She and this bloke of hers have just moved to Leeds and so I thought I'd look her up before I shoot off again."

Chloë's heart finished soaring and plummeted floorwards. "So you're not stopping in Leeds, then?"

Jack shook his head and ran his hands up and down her back. "I'm a free spirit," he said. "I go where the mood takes me. Actually, I'll probably zoom off to the ski slopes and do a stint as an instructor."

Chloë sighed. "I'll miss you," she ventured.

"So don't let's waste time fretting about that," he replied, kissing her nose and her forehead. "Just let's savour every second we have together. My darling little love."

At which point Chloë sank into his arms, closed her eyes and let the waves of sensation wash over her.

He loved her.

Jack loved her.

No one else – just her.

And nothing else in the entire universe mattered at all.

———

"You fancy Chloë, don't you?" Sinead looked Nick straight in the eyes.

"What do you mean?"

Sinead sighed to herself. He hadn't denied it. "You haven't taken your eyes off her and Jack ever since he got here," she reasoned. "The rest of us might as well be invisible."

"Sorry," he said. "Who is he, this Jack guy?"

"She met him on holiday," said Sinead. "He's a sailing instructor, I think."

Nick looked even more fed up.

"Come and have a dance," suggested Sinead boldly.

Nick sighed and shrugged. "Might as well," he said.

It was hardly the response she wanted, but at least it kept her close to him for a few minutes more.

And for now, she guessed, that was the best she could hope for.

———

"Are you going to talk to us at all tonight?" Faith asked Jasmin petulantly, when Sanjay went to collect more crisps. "Or are you going to drape yourself all over Sanjay the whole time?"

Jasmin hesitated, hearing the note of criticism in her voice.

"Are you two an item?" interjected Shelley.

"Not exactly," Jasmin replied, not wanting to tempt providence.

"So what's with all the hand-holding and dreamy looks, then?" challenged Faith. "I reckon you only wanted to get me and Shelley here so that you had an excuse to go out."

"No, honestly, I didn't," began Jasmin, as Sanjay returned with four packets of tortilla chips.

"Dance?" asked Sanjay.

"Yes please," beamed Jasmin.

She turned to Faith and Shelley. "Back in a minute," she said.

"Don't bother!" retorted Shelley. "Come on, Faith, let's go and chat to those guys in the corner." She gestured to where a group of pretty fit boys were leaning against a pillar, swaying to the music.

"I'll be over after this dance," Jasmin called after them.

"Don't bother!" Faith replied. "Go and suck up to your new friends."

———

"Come and meet all my mates," urged Chloë, dragging Jack across the room.

"This is Nick and Sinead – this is Jack. He's staying with his *sister*."

She looked pointedly at Sinead, who winked back and looked hugely relieved.

"And this is Jasmin and Sanjay."

"Hi," said Jack easily. "So you kids are all at school, yeah?"

Sinead nodded.

Nick examined the floorboards as if he hoped they would

oblige him by opening up and devouring Jack on the spot.

"That's all behind me, thank goodness," said Jack, perching on the edge of the table.

"Are you at uni?" asked Jasmin.

Jack threw back his head and roared with laughter. "You have to be joking," he said. "I could have gone, of course – in fact, I was offered three places – but I couldn't face it. Life in the great outdoors, that's more my style."

"Jack's a great sailor," said Chloë proudly. "And he's going for a job as a ski instructor this winter."

"Where?" asked Sinead.

"Swiss Alps," said Jack. "I don't suppose any of you ski?"

"Every winter since I was about ten," retorted Nick.

"Black runs?" asked Jack, inclining his head.

"No," admitted Nick. "Red mainly – and *ski de fond*, of course."

"What?"

"Cross-country," said Nick with a frown.

"Oh that," shrugged Jack. "Not enough danger in that for me. Speed skating, snowboarding, that's more my scene."

"Jack's enormously brave," interrupted Chloë. "I'd be petrified."

Jack smiled at her and patted her shoulder. "Not with me at your side," he said. "You'll have to come out, sweetheart, when I get to Val d'Isere, and let me show you the slopes."

He smiled down at Chloë. "In the meantime, let's dance." He took her hand and pulled her on to the floor.

"There's something odd about that guy," said Nick, as they drifted away.

"Oh, he's not that bad," replied Sinead, guessing he was jealous. "And he adores Chloë," she added, just to press the point home.

"Well, his geography's lousy, that's for sure," Nick went on.

Sinead frowned. "What do you mean?"

"Val d'Isere isn't in Switzerland," he replied. "It's in the French Alps."

"It's all mountains," said Sinead.

Nick looked across the room to where Jack was nibbling Chloë's left ear.

"I think," muttered Nick, as Chloë threw back her head, tossed her auburn curls and laughed into Jack's ear, "that I might very well be sick."

———

"Is that silly grin going to stay on your face all night?" teased Sinead, as her dad parked the car outside the apartment block.

Chloë laughed. "I'm just so happy," she said. "Jack said he'll phone every day and he's going to work out when he can see me again. In between job interviews and stuff," she added.

"He's a bit full of himself, isn't he?" queried Sinead.

"He's not!" retorted Chloë. "It's just that he's mature and sophisticated. Hasn't he got the most amazing eyes? And that suntan!"

"Chloë, love?"

Sinead's dad opened the car door and beckoned her out.

"Yes, Mr Flaherty?"

"Before we have another rerun of the anatomical

delights of this Jack guy, would you mind awfully if we went indoors? I've got a romantic meal to finish."

"Sorry," grinned Chloë. "Thanks for the lift. You do think he will phone, don't you, Sinead?"

"Chloë!" exclaimed Mr Flaherty. "Inside. Now."

Chapter 16

FACE TO FACE WITH HARD FACTS

FOR THE next couple of weeks, it seemed as if life might be going according to plan for all of them.

To her utmost surprise, Sinead was one of the girls Nick picked for the mixed football team. That this was largely due to the fact that three girls had chickenpox on the day of the trials and two others decided it was too cold and muddy to get involved was neither here nor there. Sinead would have played football on an ice floe if it meant being close to Nick. Chloë teased her unmercifully but she didn't care; now that Jack was on the scene, Sinead knew that Chloë would be no threat at all.

The other good thing was that her mum seemed more cheerful. She had started filling in application forms for jobs, which meant there was less time for ridiculous activities like cleaning the window frames with an old toothbrush or disinfecting the TV remote control. And her dad sold his first hand-painted table, and bought them all champagne, which made her mum go all giggly and almost like her old self. When Shaun brought home a hand-carved

Santa Claus as tall as Erin, her mum flipped straight into Christmas mode and started winding ivy round everything that didn't move. The place was beginning to look like a small rainforest but it was a small price to pay to have her mum smiling again.

The downside of all this was that Sinead's legs were covered with bruises and she was so exhausted after every football practice that she had to eat at least two chocolate bars before she could face the walk home. Thankfully Nick didn't appear to notice the zits which had started sprouting as a result – in fact, the only thing he did notice was the fact that she was what he called a pretty good dribbler for a girl.

It was, she supposed, better than nothing.

———

On a particularly cold day in early December, Jasmin had a great idea. Much as she adored Sanjay, she was getting fed up with walking the streets for two hours after school. During her IT lesson, Jasmin told Mr Buckley that she thought she needed help with her project, and that Sanjay Fraser had told her all about his ambitions and had very kindly offered to assist. It worked wonderfully; Mr Buckley said they could use the computer room until six o'clock each evening; Sanjay's hand was able to rest on her knee for long periods without interruption and when Mr Buckley was otherwise engaged, they wrote funny messages to one another on the screen or discussed the extraordinary ways in which their respective mothers were behaving.

"My mum stands in front of the mirror for ages, singing," said Jasmin one afternoon. "And every time the post comes, she grabs it and runs upstairs with it clasped to her chest. Weird or what?"

Sanjay shook his head. "Mine is the same about the post," he said. "And she's cut her hair, which drove my father crazy, and started wearing jeans. She's never worn jeans in her life."

"Mind you," said Jasmin, "it's quite good that they are going crazy."

"How come?"

"It gives them much less time to worry about what we're doing," grinned Jasmin.

———

For Nick, the best part of being in charge of the football was that it took his mind off Chloë and just what she might be doing with that Jack jerk.

He was at school by eight, cajoling his teams into an early-morning run round the playing-field, and at lunch-time and after school he was organising practices. By the time he'd finished his homework it was eleven at night and he was too tired even to dream about Chloë. Which was all for the best.

The gang hadn't been out together since the night at Fat Harry's. A couple of times he had suggested they should do something but Chloë had always said that she was already booked up.

"Jack's taking me to the cinema," she said the first time.

"Jack's taking me late-night shopping – he loves spoiling me," she said on another occasion.

And the last time it had been even worse.

"Jack wants to take me to this cool Japanese restaurant," she enthused. "He's going to buy me *sushi*."

And I hope it chokes him, Nick had thought viciously. Sadly it hadn't.

———

One Thursday, when she should have been doing a history essay and grappling with the life cycle of the amoeba, Chloë went out with Jack for the fourth time. He hadn't called her since the weekend, and she had been on the verge of despair, wondering whether he was annoyed because she had flinched at the thought of eating raw fish at The Geisha Garden and ordered an omelette instead, which he said was very unsophisticated.

But when he did ring, he explained that he had been tied up with interviews and just hadn't had the time. They went to the cinema and held hands in the double seats at the back, and he kissed her passionately and stroked her legs, and told her she set him alight. Then he took her to a pub and bought her a Blue Hawaiian, which made her knees go all funny, and then laughed at her when she couldn't walk straight on the way home. He told her about his interviews with the ski companies and when, heart in her mouth, she had asked which one he was going to take, he said he didn't want to rush into a decision, which she took to mean that he wanted to stay around her for as long as he could.

But on the following day, while she was on the bus on the way home from school with Sinead, she saw him again.

With a girl.

And it wasn't his sister.

They were standing in the doorway of a shop.

And they were kissing.

There was nothing sisterly about the kiss either.

"Just leave me alone, OK!" Chloë sobbed, running up the stairs to the apartment two at a time with Sinead hard on her heels. "Just leave me alone!"

She galloped up the final flight and rammed her key into the lock. All she wanted to do was to get to her room, shut the door and never come out again.

It was as she crossed the hall that she saw the jacket, thrown over the back of the chair, and the familiar Wallace and Gromit tie lying on the coffee table.

As she turned, she saw two big brown suitcases at the bottom of the stairs and a couple of coats slung over the bannister.

She had known all along that it would happen. And now it had.

Her mum had weakened. Dad had come home.

"Isn't this lovely, darling?" Suzy chatted nervously, her hand tightly holding on to Edward as they sat a little awkwardly, drinking mugs of tea.

"And this time things are going to be different," her father said. "I promise."

"You don't look very happy, sweetheart," ventured her mother. "Aren't you pleased that we are getting our lives back together?"

Suddenly it was all too much. Jack and the girl and now her dad being here and all the worry starting again, and Parents' Evening next week and Mrs Reilly threatening to have words, as she put it, with her mother.

"I don't care what you do!" she shouted, bursting into

tears. "Just leave me out of it, will you? Just leave me to get on with my own life!"

And while her parents stared after her, open-mouthed, she ran up to her room and slammed the door.

"Jack, oh Jack!" she sobbed. "How could you? How could you?"

———

On Saturday morning, Sinead called at the flat to see Chloë.

"Lovely to see you, dear," enthused Suzy. "We're just off out – awards ceremony in Manchester tonight, such fun – but do go up. I think," she added confidingly, "she's a bit down."

That, thought Sinead as soon as she saw Chloë, was an understatement. Her friend's eyes were puffy and bloodshot and she looked as though she hadn't slept all night.

"Hey, you!" Sinead enveloped her in a hug. "It's not the end of the world."

"And what would you know?" retorted Chloë. "You've never been in love."

Sinead thought it best not to say anything.

"So," she said firmly. "What are you going to do about it?"

"What can I do about it?" asked Chloë.

"Phone him, and demand an explanation," suggested Sinead. "No, better still – go and see him. That way, he can't hang up on you."

Chloë shook her head. "What's the point?" she said. "He's got someone else and that's an end to it."

"Chloë, that is so defeatist!" objected Sinead. "He's treated you like dirt and you can't let him get away with it. What if he does it to someone else?"

"Last time we saw him with a girl, it turned out to be his sister," Chloë ventured, clutching at straws.

"And did he look like he was kissing a sister this time?" demanded Sinead.

"No."

"Right. Get your coat."

"Pardon?"

"We are going to find Jack Kempton and get a few straight answers," asserted Sinead. "Where was it he said his sister lived? Horsforth?"

"Yes, the new Spinney Hill estate, but . . ."

"No buts," insisted Sinead. "Coat."

––––––

"Excuse me," said Sinead to an elderly man who was walking a Jack Russell terrier down Spinney Hill Road. "We're looking for a Natalie Kempton. Well, it might be Kempton, and then again it might not."

The man frowned.

"She's got a boyfriend, or maybe he's a husband," continued Sinead. "And they've only just moved in."

"Oh, that'll be the young couple in number twenty-three," he said. "Round the bend, opposite the phone box."

Sinead smiled her thanks.

"Let's leave it," begged Chloë.

"No way," said Sinead, grabbing her arm. "Look – that must be it. With the red front door."

They walked up the path and Sinead rang the bell in a determined fashion.

The door was opened by the girl they had seen in the street.

"Excuse me," said Sinead politely. "Are you Jack Kempton's sister?"

"Yes," nodded the girl, who looked a lot older without make-up and kinky boots. "Why? What's he done?"

"That," said Sinead, "is what we are here to find out."

———

"So you see," finished Sinead. "My friend is terribly upset and we think she should know the truth."

Natalie sank down in a chair and laughed.

"I don't think it's funny," retorted Sinead.

"Sinead!" Chloë was fidgeting with embarrassment.

"Sorry," Natalie said, attempting to look serious. "Of course it's not – I think I'm just laughing with relief that it isn't anything worse."

"So is Jack here?" whispered Chloë.

Natalie shook her head. "No, he's got an interview."

"We can wait," muttered Sinead.

"Another ski company?" queried Chloë.

Natalie frowned. "Excuse me?"

"He told me about these ski instructor jobs he's going after," began Chloë.

"Oh, he is a rascal!" Natalie giggled, raising her eyebrows.

"That's not what I'd call it," retorted Sinead.

Natalie swallowed. "Look, I'll make a cup of tea and then we'll talk this through. Only I think you really are overreacting."

"Tell us," said Sinead, "and then we'll be the judges of that."

———

"SINEAD!" Chloë exploded after Natalie had left the room. "How could you? You were so rude!"

"Sorry," apologised Sinead, "but I hate to see you so upset. And besides, if we don't get to the bottom of this, you'll just go on getting hurt."

Chloë smiled. "And to think a few months ago, you hated my guts," she said.

Sinead tossed her head. "You've improved," she remarked and grinned at Chloë.

———

"So you see, there will be no ski job," Natalie explained as they sipped the second cup of tea. "The only reason he was in Greece was that our uncle is manager at the sailing club and had him over for a few weeks to keep him out of trouble."

Chloë frowned. "Trouble?"

Natalie shrugged. "Not real trouble," she said. "He's just a bit of a lad – you know, flunked his A levels, bunked off college when he was supposed to be doing resits, never managed to hold down a job because he said he was bored. That sort of thing."

"But he is a good sailor," Chloë insisted.

Natalie shook her head. "He learned on the river back home as a boy," she agreed. "But he's nothing special – that's why he was only allowed to supervise the kids taking Toppers out, close to the shore. You never saw him sail anything bigger, did you?"

Chloë bit her lip. "No," she said. "But he said he skis the black runs."

Natalie raised an eyebrow. "Interesting for someone who has never been to the mountains," she muttered.

Chloë gulped.

"And this girl?" prompted Sinead.

Natalie shrugged her shoulders. "He's got several," she grinned.

Chloë choked back a sob and Sinead laid a comforting hand on her arm. "This one had short, dark hair and big boobs," she asserted.

Natalie laughed. "Oh that'll be Selena Johnson," she said. "He met her in Greece and then discovered she lives near here. That's why he wanted to come and stay with Tom and me – so that he could chat her up, he said."

"How could he!" Chloë couldn't help exclaiming. "After everything he said!"

"Oh, come on, he's just a bit of a lad," said Natalie, sipping her tea. "He's only young, after all, like you and . . ."

"Hang on!" Chloë was getting into her stride. "Just because I'm young doesn't mean I can't be up front with people. He two-timed me. What's more, he lied to me."

"Well, if you put it like that . . ."

"I do!" asserted Chloë. "How else would you like me to put it?"

It was Natalie's turn to look dejected. "You're right," she said finally, putting down her cup. "He doesn't mean any harm – he just wants people to sit up and take notice of him."

She ran her fingers through her hair. "He's the baby of the family – my mum was forty-five when he was born. He had *au pairs* and nannies and then he got packed off to boarding school when he was eight. I guess he's always been looking for someone to impress. He'll do the same with Selena Johnson, you'll see."

She sighed. "He is very ambitious, bless him," she said.

"And this place at uni?" persisted Sinead.

"What place?"

"Forget it," said Chloë, looking thoughtful.

Natalie chewed a hangnail. "I'm really sorry you've been upset, Chloë. I'll have a word with him when he gets back from this interview. Give him a bit of a ticking-off."

"No!" Chloë sounded so assertive that Sinead looked up in astonishment. "No, please don't even mention we've been here. I would really rather deal with it myself."

"Well, if you're sure . . ."

"Oh, yes, I'm sure. Absolutely positive."

"You won't be too hard on him?"

Chloë looked at her and stood up. "No harder than he has been on me," she replied.

———

"You don't honestly think that was what he was doing!" Sinead looked awestruck at the suggestion Chloë had made as they walked back to the bus stop.

"I'm certain," she said. "But sadly we have no way of proving it."

"So what are you going to do? You can't just let him get away with treating you like that."

"Oh, believe me," Chloë assured her, "I have no intention of doing that. No intention whatever."

———

"Darling, we're back!" Chloë's mum stuck her head round the bedroom door. "Are you asleep?"

"Not now," said Chloë, rolling over under the duvet and peering up at her mother. "Did you win?"

Her mother shook her head. "No, worse luck," she said. "Nathan was gutted."

"Oh good," retorted Chloë, sitting up and swinging her legs out of the bed.

"What, dear?"

"Nothing. Was Dad OK?"

"Dad was wonderful," said her mother. "He's just downstairs making some coffee. Darling, is something wrong? You look awful."

Chloë tried to smile but it didn't work.

"Oh, Mum," she sobbed. "It's been so horrible."

———

"I told you from the outset that he was no good," said her father for the third time.

"Edward . . ."

Her mother threw him a warning glance.

"You deserve better, my darling," he continued, patting her knee and plying her with hot chocolate. "I'll tell you what, why don't we all have a day Christmas shopping tomorrow? Lunch at Le Cochon Rouge, the works? What do you say?"

Chloë sniffed. He was trying to be really nice. And Mum looked so happy, despite not winning the award.

And it was up to her to build the family up again.

That was far more important than two-timing, lying, cheating boyfriends.

"That would be lovely," she said. "Really lovely."

Chapter 17

CROSS-EXAMINATION

"PROMISE ME you won't ask any stupid questions?" Sinead pleaded with her parents the following day as they walked into the school hall. "And, Dad, you won't make any silly jokes, or . . ."

"Sinead!" laughed her mother. "We're going to your Parents' Evening, not appearing on 'Newsnight'! Oh look, there's that nice Josie from the café – hi there!"

"Don't wave!" hissed Sinead. "Mum, you are so uncool!"

Mrs Flaherty glared at her and eyed her appointment card. "Come along," she said. "Mr Tompkins, Maths."

"Oh joy," muttered Sinead. "Here we go."

———

"Well, well, Mr and Mrs Fraser!" Mr Buckley beamed at Sanjay's parents and flicked through a folder. "Wonderful work from Sanjay, simply wonderful!"

"I'm very pleased to hear it," said his father. "We gather from his French and Biology teachers that his grades have been slipping somewhat."

"Only a tad," said Mr Buckley cheerfully. "I just wish all

our students were as able as Sanjay. And, after all, as long as he is hitting the A grades in the subjects he's doing for A level, that's what matters most."

Sanjay's mother frowned. "But surely, IT wasn't what we had in mind for your Advanced levels, was it, Sanjay?"

Sanjay grunted.

Mr Buckley ploughed on. "Indeed, probably not," he said. "But it's what Sanjay has in mind. 3-D animation, that's where he's heading."

"You can't be serious!"

"But I thought . . ."

Mr Buckley ignored the open-mouthed expressions on the Frasers' faces.

"Now, I have some information here!" Mr Buckley pulled some papers from his briefcase. "His best bet would be to take IT, Computer-Aided Design, and a couple of staples, Maths probably and something else that fires him up. Bristol's a good place to go, but there are others. It's all here."

"Now look here . . ." began Sanjay's father.

"I am right, aren't I, Sanjay?" Mr Buckley looked directly at Sanjay and held his gaze. "This is what you want to do with your life?"

Sanjay swallowed and glanced from his father's stern expression to his mother's bewildered one. "Yes," he said. "Yes, it is."

"Not law?" Mr Buckley persisted.

The roof of Sanjay's mouth went dry. "No," he said. "Definitely not law."

"There we are, then," said Mr Buckley decisively.

He handed Mr Fraser the folder of information, stood up

and held out his hand. "Delighted to have met you again," he enthused. "And Mrs Fraser – great potential your lad has – not surprising, with parents as successful as yourselves. But one must let them follow their star, that's what I say."

"You can't be serious!" Duncan repeated.

"I think he is, dear," said Dipti suddenly. "I have to say I'm surprised. But I think he's quite right. We all have to follow our own star. The thing about Sanjay is that he's had the guts to tell us just what that star is."

Her husband frowned. "What are you on about?"

"I'll tell you later, dear," she said. "At home. Over a stiff drink."

———

"I can't understand it, Mrs Sanderson," sighed Mrs Reilly. "Chloë is obviously very able, but this term she seems to have gone to pieces. It's not just English; I've discussed with other members of staff, and they all say the same."

Suzy slipped her hand into Chloë's. "We've had a few difficulties over the past weeks," she said hesitantly. "Nothing serious, but enough to make life very hard for Chloë."

"Ah, I see," murmured Mrs Reilly, who clearly didn't.

"I am sure that now that everything is back on an even keel, her grades will pick up. Won't they, darling?"

Chloë nodded.

"So can you tell me," said Mrs Reilly eagerly, leaning forward in a conspiratorial manner, "what the problem was?"

"No," said Suzy. "I can't."

"Oh," said Mrs Reilly. "Next!"

"A lovely girl, Mr and Mrs Johnson! You must be so proud of her!"

Mrs Braithwaite's ample bosom leaped about enthusiastically.

"We are," agreed Harry and Josephine in unison.

You could have fooled me, thought Jasmin, wriggling with embarrassment.

"Her grasp of History is excellent and she is so conscientious. Of course, the fact that she has such a lovely group of friends must have helped her to settle down here at Lockbridge High."

"See?" she couldn't help muttering.

"We're thrilled that she's involved in this football competition," said Josephine. "Quite a new thing for Jasmin."

Jasmin gulped and Mrs Braithwaite frowned. "Are you, dear? I didn't see your name on the team list."

"I – um, well the thing is . . . I was, but I've dropped out."

"You never said," remarked her father.

"It didn't seem important," shrugged Jasmin.

"We'll talk about it later," said her mother. "I really think you should keep it up – it seems like such a wholesome activity."

Another excuse bites the dust, thought Jasmin. The problem is, where do we go from here?

———

"I'm so proud of you!" Nick's mum enveloped him in a hug.

"MUM! Let go!" Nick wriggled out of her clasp. "People will look."

"Sorry," she laughed. "But the headmaster was so complimentary about your work, and the football and everything. Your dad would have been so thrilled."

Nick swallowed. "Would he? Really?"

"Nick, he'd have been over the moon. You know what he used to say. 'Sock it to them!' And believe me, you have!"

Nick grinned. "Thanks," he said. "Can we get fish and chips on the way home?"

His mother roared with laughter and Nick had the rather pleasant feeling that he was, really this time, beginning to get over it a bit.

And then he caught sight of Chloë and sighed.

There were some things he would never get over.

———

"Have you thought what to do about Jack?" hissed Sinead to Chloë as their respective parents stood chatting at the school gates.

"I'm getting there," said Chloë. "I need to go out with him once more . . ."

"Chloë!"

"It's OK," Chloë assured her. "I'll get him to come out with the gang. That should do it."

"What are you on about?"

"Wait and see," said Chloë.

———

"You've written a *what*?" Duncan Fraser gripped his whisky and water and stared at his wife.

"A romantic novel," Dipti repeated, holding her head high.

"Brilliant!" breathed Sanjay.

"Does that mean Mummy's clever?" asked Rani.

"Very," grinned Sanjay.

"I've taken characters from Indian legends, translated them to Twenty-first Century Britain and devised a few plot-lines based on mythology. Cool or what?"

"Oh for pity's sake!" retorted her husband. "You're sounding like some empty-headed teenager now. And what about your academic work?"

"Stuff my academic work!" she retorted. "I need a new challenge . . ."

"Some challenge!" interjected Duncan. "Frivolous, empty-headed rubbish!"

"You haven't read it, Dad," reasoned Sanjay.

"I don't need to," grunted his father.

"I can't read very well," said Rani sadly.

"You're getting better all the time," said Sanjay.

His father stood up. "Of course, it's unlikely to be accepted," he said. "And if it is, of course, you won't put your own name on it."

Dipti stared at him. And then at Sanjay.

"Yes, I will," she said.

Duncan gasped.

"I wasn't going to," she admitted. "I was going to call myself Venetia Valentine."

Sanjay spluttered into his hot chocolate. "Oh puh-leese!" he said.

"But that Mr Buckley was right," she went on. "You have to follow your own star and you have to have the courage of your convictions."

She sipped her coffee. "Hey!" she said suddenly. "Who knows? One day Sanjay might make a 3-D film of my book!"

"Cool!" said Sanjay.

"I love films," purred Rani.

"This entire family," grunted Duncan, "has gone stark raving mad."

———

"I never was in the team."

Jasmin waited for the parental explosion.

"I guessed as much," said her mother, calmly dropping tea bags into the pot.

"Why did you lie?" demanded her father. "What was the point?"

"Sanjay was the point," said Josephine. "And it was my fault."

Jasmin gasped. "You knew?"

"I worked it out on the way home," confessed her mother. "I disapproved of Sanjay, you were determined to see him and the football competition gave you the necessary alibi. Am I right?"

Jasmin nodded. "I didn't mean to lie to you," she said. "But Sanjay's a really nice guy. And you made like I was about to elope with him or something. He's a friend – a really close friend. And I can't see that his race or his nationality matters."

Her father looked worried. "You're very young," he began.

"Dad, I am almost sixteen," said Jasmin. "Old enough to make my own decisions. Old enough to throw away outdated prejudices."

Her parents were speechless.

Which, thought Jasmin, was something of a triumph in itself.

Chapter 18

SORTED? OR NOT?

"About christmas," said Chloë's father over breakfast on Tuesday. "I thought we could book into a hotel somewhere, just the three of us!"

"We can't do that!" Chloë exclaimed. " I want to be with my friends."

"And besides, dear," ventured Suzy, "we'd never get in anywhere now – and the Reeds have invited us for Boxing Day."

"What, Slimeball?" asked Chloë.

"Who?"

"Nathan." Chloë corrected herself. "Is he married?"

"Of course he is," said Suzy. "His wife's Harriet Dupont, the violinist. She's just back from a tour of South Africa."

"I don't much fancy that," said her father hastily.

"Me neither," added Chloë. I don't trust that guy, she thought.

Suzy dabbed her mouth with a napkin and poured some more coffee. "Then the Pritchards are having open house on Christmas Eve . . ."

"Who?" Edward looked irritated.

"Ellen and Lionel," Suzy said. "She did all the set design for my show."

"Look!" Edward threw his napkin on to the table and stood up. "Can we for once do something that has absolutely nothing to do with bloody Pennine TV!"

Chloë froze.

Suzy paled.

"Dad!"

Edward sank back down into his chair. "Sorry," he said more softly. "I'm sorry. I just think that a nice hotel somewhere in the Lakes, or Scotland, maybe would be best."

Suzy nodded and fixed a bright smile on her lips. "Great idea," she said. "The more I think about it, the more I like it. What do you say, Chloë?"

"Fine," Chloë replied.

What else was there to say? She had to do what would be best for her mother.

———

"I got it! I got it! I got it! Oh my heavens! Oh lordy, lordy, lordy!"

Josephine Johnson grabbed Jasmin by the arm and began waltzing round the café to the extreme amusement of two businessmen who were ploughing their way through the Bumper Bahamian Breakfast.

"MUM!" Jasmin gasped. "What on earth has happened?"

Josie waved a sheet of paper in the air. "The Northern Gospel Singers – they advertised for contraltos – and I auditioned. And I'm in!!!"

"That's great," smiled Jasmin. "Is it like the choir you went to when we lived in London?"

"Bigger, much bigger," said Josie, grinning from ear to ear. "They've been on TV and radio."

"Cool," said Jasmin.

"And they do tours all over the place – not just in the UK, but France, Italy, America even."

"But you can't go off and leave us!" exploded Jasmin.

Josie stopped twirling, stuffed the letter in her pocket and affectionately pinched Jasmin's nose. "Just watch me, sweetheart," she grinned. "Just watch me!"

———

"But, Josie, you can't!" Harry was so stunned that he dropped a whole tray of kumquats on the kitchen floor. "I mean, how will I cope without you?"

Josephine ruffled his grey, curly hair affectionately. "Harry, I'm not emigrating," she laughed. "I'm simply doing what I've wanted to do for years."

"But this place won't run itself," insisted Harry.

"Which is why we will promote Jenny," said Josephine triumphantly. "Make her manageress – after all, she's the one with all the bright ideas and the enthusiasm."

Harry looked thoughtful. "She is good," he said. "And the customers adore her."

"That's that, then!" said Josie triumphantly. "But we will have to pay her more."

"That's OK," said Harry. "She's worth it. And Josie?" Harry took her hand.

"Yes?"

"I'm really proud of you," he said, kissing her on the lips.

"And I'm proud of you, too, darling," she whispered. "This place will be the hottest spot in Leeds before long, and it's all down to you."

"You sound as if you quite like it after all," grinned Harry.

"Oh, I do," smiled Josie. "I love it to bits now I know I don't have to be here all the time!"

———

"Me? Manageress? Oh thank you, Harry, thank you, thank you!"

Jenny wrapped her arms round Harry's stocky body and planted a kiss on his cheek.

"I won't let you down, I promise!" she said. "And you know, I've been thinking – we ought to have a big Valentine's Day promotion, and maybe a SpringFest, like they do on the Continent. I've read about it."

"Jenny!" laughed Harry.

"Yes?"

"Could we just sort Christmas out first?"

Jenny laughed. "Leave it to me," she said. "Consider it sorted."

———

"My mother has gone stark raving mad," sighed Sinead at lunch-time.

"What took her so long?" grinned Chloë. "Mine's been dotty for ages."

"It must be something in the air," agreed Jasmin. "Mine's planning to desert her family and warble her way around the world."

"Mine," said Sinead, "has transformed our flat into some

sort of fairy grotto. We've got nodding Father Christmasses, musical bells over the doorways, whole trees painted silver in the sitting-room and a reindeer that says 'Fly with me' when you prod its horns. And there's still two weeks to go."

"I used to love Christmas," said Jasmin. "But this year I guess the place will be full of customers and I'll have to play the charming daughter."

"I'm going to be at the café for Christmas lunch," said Nick. "What's more, your mum said she'd pay me to help in the kitchen when it's busy."

"Cool," said Jasmin. "That means she has to pay me too – equality and all that."

"I could help too," interjected Sinead eagerly. "It would be fun."

"We could all do it," agreed Sanjay.

"I'll be away," sighed Chloë. "Best behaviour in some glitzy hotel."

"Great!" enthused Sinead. "I mean, it sounds lovely."

"So you won't be around?" asked Nick.

Chloë shook her head sorrowfully.

There was no need, thought Sinead, for Nick to look quite so downcast.

———

"So come on! What shall we do as an end-of-term bash?"

Jasmin speared a fish-finger with her fork.

"Bowling?" suggested Sanjay.

"Boring," said Sinead.

"Go-karting?" asked Nick.

"Get lost," retorted Jasmin.

"I know," said Chloë suddenly. "Ice-skating."

"Yes!" Nick punched the air and then looked away shamefacedly. "I mean, that sounds like the right sort of Christmassy thing to do," he waffled.

"I'll invite Jack," added Chloë.

"Oh," said Nick.

"I have a few scores to settle," she murmured through gritted teeth.

Nick perked up and looked at her in an enquiring manner.

"I do wish," she mused, "that we hadn't lost my e-mail. I could really put paid to his schemes if I had it."

Nick almost leaped out of his seat. "Where did you lose it?"

"I didn't lose it, silly," said Chloë. "It got trashed. By Jasmin's mother. I never even got to see it."

Sanjay ripped the ring-pull off a can of lemonade. "Are you sure it's gone?" he asked calmly. "Have you double-checked the wastebasket?"

"Mum said she had destroyed it," Jasmin told him.

"I doubt she got rid of it completely," replied Sanjay. "She probably just binned it and it's still sitting in the wastebasket. Everyone always forgets to empty that – we have hundreds of old messages in ours at home. Why don't we take a look tonight?"

"No! That is . . ." Jasmin faltered.

Sanjay touched her hand. "Jasmin, I can't hide from your mum for ever."

Jasmin swallowed. "OK," she whispered. "Come after school. Mum will be at choir. Come to think of it, maybe this singing lark is not such a bad idea after all."

———

"See?" Sanjay said triumphantly. "There it is! Still sitting in the wastebasket."

"Right. Let me see!" ordered Chloë.

Hi, Sexy Lady!
Remember the wonderful time we had?
How we danced cheek to cheek at the disco? How
you laughed at that weird movie? Remember the
way we kissed?

"Movie? We didn't see any movies," muttered Chloë.

She scanned the rest of the e-mail.

"*Well, I've got a surprise for you,*" she read. "*And this time, we'll make sure we don't get lost.*"

She looked at Sinead. "We never got lost," she said. "I knew it. That e-mail was never meant for me."

Sanjay peered at the screen. "It's got Jasmin's e-mail address on," he said. "Johnson-at-cancaf-dot-uk."

"Then Jack sent it to the wrong address," said Chloë. "Remember, Sinead, that his sister told us the girl he was going out with was called Selena Johnson."

"Yes, so what . . . oh!"

"He obviously got her e-mail address and Jasmin's muddled because it was the same surname. Now I know why he seemed so confused when I mentioned receiving it. It was all just another lie."

"Do you want me to print it out?" asked Sanjay.

"No," said Chloë firmly. "Delete it. Properly, this time. Jack Kempton is history. Or will be after Saturday night."

"He's coming!" Chloë banged the phone down and grinned at Sinead in satisfaction.

"Is he meeting us at the rink?"

"Oh no," said Chloë. "I told him to meet us at the bus station. That way, he has no escape."

"Chloë, just what are you up to?" asked Sinead.

"Wait and see," said Chloë.

———

"Hi there!" Sanjay waved to Nick, Sinead and Jasmin, who were waiting in the foyer of the ice rink.

Jasmin gasped. He wasn't alone.

"This is Rani," said Sanjay. "My sister. My parents had to go out and the baby-sitter cancelled, so she's come to watch, haven't you, Rani?"

"Come to watch," nodded Rani. "Hello."

Jasmin tried not to look at her. "Hi," she said and hurried over to the video machines.

"Hello," said Sinead, smiling at Rani. "Would you like a drink while we wait?"

"Can it be a very fizzy one?"

Sinead laughed. "I shall see to it personally!"

She took Rani's hand.

"Where's Chloë?" Nick scanned the foyer of the ice rink.

"She's on her way," sighed Sinead. "She has something to attend to. Come on, Rani!"

The two of them headed for the soft drinks bar.

"She's so excited," Sanjay said to Jasmin. "She's never been to an ice rink before."

"You should have told me you were bringing her!" said Jasmin accusingly. "I wasn't prepared!"

Sanjay frowned. "Prepared for what?"

"Well, you know – I mean, what do you say to them? What do they understand?"

Sanjay closed his eyes for a moment and bit his lip. "Jasmin, she's a little girl. Treat her like any other little girl. Pretend she's nine instead of thirteen and you're home and dry."

Jasmin looked doubtful. "Should you have brought her to a place like this?" she asked. "I mean, people might stare."

"Let them!" snapped Sanjay. "I can't believe you said that."

"I didn't mean it like that . . ."

"Look," he said more calmly. "You complain because your mum doesn't want you to go out with me because I'm not African-Caribbean . . ."

"I never said that!"

"You didn't have to," he said. "Chloë explained."

"I'll kill her!" said Jasmin.

"What for? Telling the truth?" Sanjay enquired. "Anyway, you say your mum is prejudiced."

"She is!"

"No more than you," reasoned Sanjay. "You don't know Rani, you've never spoken to her. Don't judge her by her appearance, or her mental age. Judge her for what she is."

Jasmin looked at the ground. "I'll try," she murmured. "Can we skate now?"

———

"Darling!" Jack kissed Chloë and slipped his hand into hers. "Coffee? Drink? Cinema?"

Chloë smiled up at him sweetly. "No thanks," she said. "It's my turn to treat you."

Jack looked surprised. "So where are we going?"

"You'll see," said Chloë. "I just know you're going to love it."

"Of course I am, sweetheart!" said Jack. "I'm with you."

For now, thought Chloë. But not for long.

———

"Skating!" Jack stood in the foyer of the rink with a frown on his face. "With all your mates?"

Chloë nodded. "I knew how much you'd love it," she said. "And I did so want it to be a special evening."

"Right," he said hesitantly.

"You get the skates over here," said Chloë, waving across to where the others were standing lacing up their boots. "Come on."

"Well, I don't know whether . . ."

"Of course, you'll be brilliant at it compared with the rest of us," she said. "You said speed skating was your thing. I can't wait to see you in action."

Jack said nothing but his face went as white as a sheet.

"Jack?"

Chloë stared at him, unsmiling.

"I'll be with you in a moment," he said. "You go on ahead."

"Oh no," said Chloë firmly. "I'll wait until you are ready."

———

Jasmin tottered on to the ice.

"Will you hold my hand?" she begged Sanjay.

"Try stopping me," he grinned as they wobbled off. "Stay there, Rani, and watch!"

"You're amazing!" Nick exclaimed, as Sinead executed a dainty little jump and turn and began skating backwards. "It's as much as I can do to stay upright."

"I'll hold your hand if you like," suggested Sinead.

"OK, then, thanks," said Nick. "But I don't want to slow you down."

"Oh you won't," Sinead asssured him. "You won't slow me down at all."

———

"Would you like a go, Rani?" Sinead asked as she skated to the edge.

"Can't do it," said Rani sadly.

"You could try, if I held you very tight," said Sinead.

Rani's face creased into one great grin. "Yes," she nodded. "Try please."

———

Sanjay stopped in the middle of the rink and paused for breath.

"Sinead's ever so good with her," he commented. "Only I think I had better go and help – Rani needs someone either side." He began to skate off.

"No!" said Jasmin, taking a deep breath. "You carry on skating. I'll go."

"Are you sure?"

Jasmin nodded. "I need to get to know her," she said. "And there's no time like the present."

"Thanks," said Sanjay. And Jasmin knew he meant it.

———

"Actually, I think I'll give this a miss," Jack said to Chloë when she and Sinead urged him yet again to get on the ice. "The thing is, I think I've pulled a muscle in my groin which is preventing me from . . ."

"Forget it, Jack!" Sinead interrupted.

"We know, Jack," added Chloë. "About the fact that you can't skate, that you've never skied in your life, that you haven't got a job in the Alps and that you are a two-timing liar."

Jack's face flushed scarlet. "I don't know what you're talking about . . ." he began.

"We're talking," said Chloë, "about the fact that Val d'Isere is in the French Alps, not the Swiss . . ."

"You knew!" gasped Nick.

". . . and that the e-mail you sent to me was meant for Selena Johnson!"

This time Jack went pale. "Who told you?"

"I think," said Chloë, "that you and I had better have a chat. You can buy me a double hot chocolate while we talk."

———

"I like you," Rani told Sinead after she had settled her down with a bag of tortilla chips and a milk-shake. "You could come to my party if you like, only it's been stopped."

"Stopped?"

Sanjay smiled. "The special school she goes to has lost five volunteers in one term," he said. "Lots of the kids need one-to-one supervision, so most of the fun activities are on hold. They don't even go swimming these days, because they don't have enough helpers."

"Don't like swimming," shivered Rani. "Cold and wet.

Like parties, though. A lot."

Sinead looked thoughtful. "And people volunteer? They don't have to take money?"

Sanjay sighed. "No, the helpers are all unpaid," he said. "The school can't afford to pay the number of assistants they need. That's the problem."

Sinead grinned broadly. "I don't think so," she replied. "Quite the opposite. I think it's the solution."

———

"It was only a bit of holiday fun," reasoned Jack.

"I thought," said Chloë, "that you cared about me."

"I did," he said. "I do."

His eyes didn't meet hers.

"No, Jack, you only care about yourself," said Chloë calmly. "And all those lies – why?"

Jack bit his lip. "Life sucks," he said shortly. "Nothing you want to happen ever does, so you might as well have a laugh and make the best of it. There's no harm done."

"Actually you're right," said Chloë. "There would have been a lot more harm done if I hadn't found out about you. I might have got quite fond of you."

Jack laughed nervously. "That's it, you see," he said. "I'm not up for commitment and all that stuff. Easy come, easy go, that's me."

"So go," said Chloë.

"What – now?"

"If not sooner," retorted Chloë.

———

"Are you OK?" Sinead took Chloë's arm.

Chloë nodded and wiped away a stray tear. "Apart from

feeling the biggest idiot on earth," she said. "Why was I so gullible? Why did I believe him?"

"Because you wanted to," said Sinead. "We all do crazy things when we're in love. Like busting a gut on a football pitch when all you really want to do is curl up by the fire."

Chloë giggled. "Come on," she said. "Let's all skate."

———

Sinead was in seventh heaven. Nick had clutched on to her hand for ages and now he was following her round and round the rink as she twirled, executing figures of eight and generally doing all in her power to hold his attention.

And then it happened. One minute Nick and Sinead and Chloë were fooling around, playing an utterly childish game of Ring-a-Roses, and the next Sinead was screaming in agony.

"What happened?" Nick dropped down on to one knee.

"It's my ankle," she sobbed. "I've twisted it."

Sanjay skated across with Rani clutching his hand.

"Poor girl," said Rani, stroking Sinead's hair. "Rani make it all better."

Sinead blinked and tried to smile. "Do you know how to undo laces, Rani?" she asked.

Rani nodded. "I'm good with laces," she said proudly, taking hold of one lace.

"I'll do it," said Chloë.

"No," said Sinead. "Let Rani. Please."

She flinched with pain.

"Hold my hand," said Nick. "If it helps."

"It helps," said Sinead and passed out.

———

"Feeling better, darling?" Kathleen Flaherty put an arm round Sinead as she came out of the anaesthetic.

Sinead smiled wearily. "Mmm," she said. "I've found you a job."

"Sorry?"

Her mum looked confused.

"Rani-watching," said Sinead and promptly fell asleep.

The nurse smiled at Kathleen. "Don't worry," she said. "They often talk nonsense after an op."

———

"Well," said Nick the following day, as they all sat on the end of Sinead's bed. "I've heard of excuses for getting out of football practice, but this beats the lot!"

Sinead grinned ruefully. "I guess I'm out of the team," she said. "The doctor says it's a bad break and I'll be on crutches for a few weeks. And I was so looking forward to it."

Chloë spluttered into her hand.

Nick nodded. "You could organise a team of cheerleaders," he suggested. "Morale must be kept up – it's crucial."

"Brilliant," breathed Sinead, who knew nothing about cheerleading but was rapidly warming to the idea of boosting Nick's morale.

"I don't suppose you'd like to take Sinead's place?" he suggested to Chloë.

Sinead held her breath.

"Get real!" laughed Chloë. "I can't think of anything I'd like less!"

Sinead exhaled with relief.

"By the way," asked Sanjay, "what happened to Jack? He disappeared pretty early last night."

"Jack," said Chloë through gritted teeth, "is a geek."

"He is?" Nick nearly fell off the end of Sinead's bed.

"A total dweeb," added Sinead. "Chloë doesn't need him. In fact," she added with a grin, "she doesn't need anyone else when she has us lot!"

"Definitely!" said Jasmin.

"Right on," agreed Sanjay.

"Exactly," stressed Nick, gazing directly at Chloë, who was beginning to look a little pink.

"Right," said Sinead, grinning at them all. "That's that sorted then. Anyone got any chocolate?"

BEST FRIENDS – TOGETHER

Who'd have thought that Chloë – cool, rich and *so*
sophisticated – would have anything in common with
Sinead, who longs for popularity?

And who'd have suspected the problems lurking
beneath Jasmin's sparkling smile? And if we're talking
about mysteries, then just who is Nick – the fit, supercool
guy, but what is he hiding?

And what of Sanjay, who finds his computer so much
more user-friendly than people?

As five very different teenagers struggle to cope
with their changing lives they fall into a friendship which
surprises them all . . .

*". . . five teenagers from very different backgrounds, the fun
and drama of their lives is drawn with humour and sensitivity."*
Pick of the Paperbacks, THE BOOKSELLER

If you would like more information about books
available from Piccadilly Press and how to order
them, please contact us at:

**Piccadilly Press Ltd
5 Castle Road
London
NW1 8PR**

Fax: 0171 267 4493